DRAGON KIN

Maria E. Schneider

Bear Mountain Books

A Bear Mountain Books Production
www.BearMountainBooks.com

Maria E. Schneider

Printing History:
POD printing November 2015
POD printing January 2018

Cover Art: Background elements of the cover from depositphotos.com

Dragon: Copyright 2017 Stanley Morrison www.stanleymorrisonart.com

ISBN-10: 0692580948
ISBN-13: 978-0692580943 (Bear Mountain Books)

Acknowledgments

For the cows, I thank Frank Tuttle. No, the story doesn't have cows, but it was an admirable suggestion that helped with a case of writer's block. I dropped dragons and snakes in instead. For the gargoyles, I thank April. No, the story doesn't have them either, but it probably should. To all my fans, thank you. Thanks to beta readers Dee and Old Granny. You deserve dragons of your own.

And thanks to my husband who puts up with cows, dragons, gargoyles and other ideas that float around this house like dust bunnies. Oh, wait. Those *are* dust bunnies!

Chapter 1

Just about the last thing I needed was a baby dragon. Obviously investigating the pitiful crying coming from the ravine had been a mistake, but I'd hoped to find an easy meal or, failing that, put a suffering animal out of its misery. I wasn't hungry or stupid enough to eat a dragon and this one, having just hatched, was too small anyway. The still soft scales were a damp pewter with flashes of iridescent silvery blue. It gobbled the shells around it, snuffling for something more nutritious even as it polished off the hard shell bits.

The warbling cries between bites were no doubt a call for Mom Dragon, but from the torn bushes, felled tree and drag marks, I had a very bad feeling that Mom wasn't able to answer. The stench in the pocket of earth reeked of blood and sulfuric fumes.

The baby was not much bigger than a fluffy duckling, but rounder with a pointed snout and a spiked tail. Now that the border to Wendal had opened to commerce, everyone knew Wendal contained dragons. I just hadn't expected to stumble across one so soon, especially such a new entrant to the world.

I tossed it a piece of jerky from my pack. "You look to be in a bit of a spot." And that meant I was in one now too.

The dragon snatched up the jerky, swallowing it in one gulp. The resulting puff of smoke and cough might have been a complaint meant to let me know it preferred fresh food, most likely raw. "I don't have any rabbits," I said.

It perked up at the mention of possible food and hurried my way on legs that were much too fast and steady for such a round creature. It should have been ungainly, but the thing was like an arrow, straight and quick, its feet light across the debris littering the ground.

The baby was hardly a danger to me so I fished out another piece of jerky. My supply was very low. I gnawed off half a bite for myself before tossing the rest to the dragon.

His mournful peep informed me of his disappointment, but he ate the food anyway.

A shout from somewhere above the lip of the ravine had me kneeling quickly to get out of sight. The dragon took my actions as an invitation and hopped on my shoulder.

"Shh," I admonished, almost silently. The shout had been a ways off; there was time.

I turned to make my way back up the opposite slope. The dragon squawked a low protest in my ear and nipped at the straggles of brown hair that had escaped my messy braid. The little hatchling flew from my shoulder, landing near one of the trees that had lost a limb or two in the recent fight. There was no point in warning the dragon that I couldn't afford to wait. I kept walking, but backwards to keep it in sight as long as possible.

At first I thought the hatchling had gone back for a last bit of eggshell, but then I recognized the shape it was tugging at was a human hand attached to an arm.

"Blast it all." Keeping low, I hurried over.

The news was not pretty and worse, not moving. The man was dressed in unique brownish-gold and white leathers that almost resembled fur. He was out cold. The lump on his forehead was half as big as the baby dragon and bleeding. His arm was broken and blood smeared across his ribs.

"We need to go," I muttered. Maybe the person who had shouted was leaving, not approaching. My frantic inspection of the hidden enclave saw no reward for returning here except the tiny dragon, which had been an egg until a few minutes ago.

Did the voice know about the man in the bushes who wasn't quite dead? Was the voice coming back to finish him off?

Of course, if someone had dragged away a mother dragon, he might well come back for an egg.

The baby dragon pulled relentlessly on the man's finger, moving it a full two inches. No way could the dragon carry this guy. "Rotting bag of chicken crap."

I slung my pack sideways, not worried about losing it because it was tied around my waist. Kneeling, I shoved the guy against the nearest tree. The eight-inch dragon grasped the guy's cape in his teeth, hopping along with one corner of it.

"That'll help." If I ever needed the dragon to pull a cape over my eyes, we were in business.

Once against the tree, I worked the stranger's upper body over my shoulder. My five-foot-four inch frame nearly buckled when I tried to stand. It wouldn't have worked, except for the incline which allowed gravity to pull him in the right direction.

The crack of a stick told me we were out of time.

If the dragon hadn't squawked and flown in the direction of the noise, I'd have dropped the guy and opted to run or fight. Since the stub of a dragon seemed concerned about the injured man, it wasn't likely bailing on us now, but there was no time to figure out details.

With as loudly as I was breathing to make it up the incline, the words between the two approaching men were mostly lost.

"Is that the dragon spawn? Get the dragonsbane!"

"It was a bird, you asshole."

The two voices wasted time arguing, drowning out my desperate pants. Once up the short but steep side, toting my burden was much easier, more like being buried alive without the fight. The guy over my shoulder had to weigh fourteen or fifteen stone. It probably wasn't doing his head any good to be upside down over my shoulder either, but the two men behind me likely had worse plans for him if they found him.

"Just give me the dragonsbane, idiot!"

Wolfsbane was used to poison wolves. The name "dragonsbane" didn't bode well for the new hatchling. "Little dragon, you had better fly."

My lungs twisted and cramped as though I were trying to swallow them instead of merely use them to breathe. I kept huffing, not worried about being silent because staying upright took all my energy.

A flash of color to my right resolved itself into tiny claws clutching at my shoulder. The dragon hissed in my ear. If it was telling me to go faster, it was out of luck.

"Gone!" I heard behind me. The shout wasn't as loud as expected, but the men were now down in the ravine while I was not. There was no way to know if they were talking about the baby dragon or the man being gone, but either way, I doubted they would forgo a search.

We were in trouble. Outrunning them would be easy without my burden.

Well then, I'd have to get rid of him, baby dragon complaints or no.

I headed for the river I had crossed earlier that morning. At a brisk walk it was less than an hour away. If I jogged, I could cut that time in half. There hadn't been any nice, hidden caves or burrows along the way, and the deer paths I had traveled mostly avoided thick undergrowth. Hiding came naturally to me, but it wouldn't be possible to disappear with a heavy person draped over my back.

I swerved in and around trees, taking hits from branches. If I had half my grandmother's gift, the trees would avoid me and tangle the undergrowth behind me on command. Instead of Grandmother, I was stuck with a newborn dragon. "Find deep woods," I gasped out in a hushed whisper. "Or a cave or vines or brambles. Hurry."

The dragon either understood, or he had to take a pee, or who knows, maybe he finally decided we humans weren't worth his little life. If I had wings...

Sweat dripped into my eyes, and the pack hanging from my waist caught on every available branch, bush and twig. I finally managed to sling it in front of me while still forcing my legs forward.

"Don't go lighting the dragonsbane until we have it in sight! The wind is up. If you waste the stuff while it's sitting in a tree upwind, we'll never capture it."

They were catching up fast.

I nearly fell over backwards when the dragon flashed in front of my eyeballs, puffing a foul smoke right into my nose. He flew to the side.

I swerved with a grunt. There was no time to reorient myself. My feet were faster than my eyes, and I was knee deep in a pile of leaves before I could slow down. The rotting log underneath me gave way, but my forward momentum slammed my shins into the far side of the buried log.

I pitched forward, my burden flipping over and off my shoulders. At least the guy softened my landing. If it hadn't been for my shins jamming into the log, I'd have been uninjured.

The dragon fluttered in front of my eyeballs, squawking quiet little peeps like an enraged hummingbird.

Voices.

They were within a few trees.

I sat up and shoved leaves over the still form of my burden. His head was hidden behind what was left of the log so there was no need to cover it. When I took a final scan, his amber eyes were open, staring at me with the intensity of a hunter. His brows drew together in confusion or anger. Before he could speak I pressed my finger to his lips and leaned in close. "Stay still and quiet. They are coming."

Thankfully his pants were browns and beige, whatever the material. He looked just like another pile of leaves the way the light reflected off him. Good enough.

I took off at a dead run, making as much noise as possible.

Chapter 2

Running should have been easier now, but I was out of breath from trying to carry something nearly twice my own weight. My shins probably hurt, but the pain in my lungs and shoulder kept me from feeling much else. The sweet scent of water was easier for me to smell than for most people, and running hard didn't alter that fact. I kept putting one foot in front of the other and continued to head for the river.

It took me a few yards to slip into a practiced stride. I automatically quieted my headlong rush. The men following had enough clues to keep them on my trail unless they tripped over the same log I had and landed in the injured guy's lap.

The dragon either stayed with the injured guy or otherwise disappeared. He could have acted as a last second distraction, but with dragonsbane involved, he was much better off hiding. There were no dragons in Anton where I had resided all my life, at least not any known ones. My scant knowledge of the scaled beasts had been gleaned from a single traveler who had taken lodging with Uncle Ralph for a fortnight and the two books I filched from my father's old library. Dragonsbane hadn't been mentioned at all, in either case.

Something had certainly felled a large mom dragon and allowed her to be dragged away. One of the voices had mentioned the wind direction. Did dragonsbane involve a strong scent? Or were they planning on burning the stuff?

I kept to my steady jog, considering my options. I could lose the men pretty quickly if it became absolutely necessary, but if they were to backtrack too soon, they might stumble across the injured man. The water wasn't too far. If I could make it there and then disappear, they wouldn't likely hunt back along the entire trek.

From the crashing, cursing and snapped branches behind me, the two were large men. My current nimble pace kept them at bay, but they refused to lose ground. I darted sideways to avoid running across a clearing. The open meadow provided too much opportunity for arrows or other thrown weapons. They were close enough that a glimpse would make it obvious there was one of me, and I was neither the injured man nor the dragon they sought.

To my dismay, they wasted no time tracing my footsteps around the clearing. Either they were used to tracking or simply guessed I had taken the longer route around. Their intelligence was dangerous and hinted that, smell it or not, they knew the river was ahead.

No wonder they weren't desperate to close the distance. Once I hit the river, they could box me in against bad terrain or swampy mud.

Well, too bad they didn't know I intended to swim. I bundled my cloak into a ball and tied it around my pack without breaking stride. The pack was nearly watertight.

A few paces from the water I picked up speed, running full out, letting my breath come as hard and loud as it liked. I was thirsty anyway, and they had pushed dangerously close.

I barely had enough time for a deep breath before slicing into the water, arms and head first, my pack fighting the clean, shallow dive, but then helping me sink as soon as I was submerged.

I replaced running with kicking, pushing my body down and out into the middle of the river. At the same time, I used my grandmother's gift, sending hollow wooden limbs from my nose and mouth to the surface. The tubes were dense enough to keep water from seeping in and provided me with wonderful, lovely fresh air. I was breathing so hard, it was a miracle the hollow branches didn't whistle like bagpipes.

Even knowing the oxygen was available, claustrophobia threatened to panic me. The river water was a murky brownish-green with debris and darting fish bodies. When the deeper currents began to carry me along there was more light available, but not much to see.

I panted hard through the hollow branches, struggling through a gasp when water splashed into the openings. It was far too early to consider emerging so I swallowed bits of water and kept on swimming.

The shouting on the riverbank was easy to hear, but the words were nothing but distorted bellows. The men were no longer a worry. If they waited for me to come up for air, they would wait forever.

I kept one arm tight across my pack and paddled just enough to keep me low in the water. I was nothing but a fading ripple being carried quickly downstream.

Chapter 3

Truthfully, letting the river carry me for a while was a nice respite. Escaping had exhausted my reserves, and having just traveled for three weeks on foot, I was far from fully rested anyway. A nap would have been possible had I not been worried about drowning.

Leaving the river was almost too much work. I was soaked, tired and hungry. With two or so hours to sunset, there might be time to find shelter or food, but probably not both. I was also lost, but that didn't particularly bother me. My goal when I left Anton was to make sure no one could find me. If I didn't know where I was, it wasn't likely anyone else would know either.

I had wasted a lot of time doubling back in the past two weeks, covering my trail and stopping in towns to see if news of my disappearance had spread. Uncle Ralph kept it completely quiet for the first week; after all, he wasn't keen to admit his eldest niece had taken flight right after her nuptials were announced. Unbeknownst to him, dear Grandmother Burgundy had provided me warning two days earlier, and I was gone long before the public announcement.

There was no point in arguing with my uncle. Despite the fact that his brother had raised independent daughters, Uncle failed to notice our abilities or intelligence. We were nothing more than a convenience that kept the castle running smoothly, and now, apparently, we were to be auctioned off for his gain.

Uncle Ralph's two biggest concerns in life were to gain control of the monies we inherited when our father died and to gain a title from the king. Sadly for him, Grandmother had squirreled away the fortune that he expected to control upon taking us into his household. And anything Grandmother hid stayed that way.

Of course, if Uncle found out that Grandmother had overheard the nuptial plans and warned me, he would chop her into so many pieces...I stopped that unpleasant thought. Grandmother could take care of herself. If the situation became any more desperate, she'd uproot and take Ava and hide so deep in a forest no one would find them.

I hoped.

I had begged her to leave with me, but she wanted me safely away while Uncle was still unsuspecting. It was a logical plan, but that didn't mean

I liked it.

I stared into the trees, too tired to hunt. Fishing was easier than hunting rabbits. I had twine, and bait would be easy enough to find in the mud along the bank.

My cloak was patchwork leather and lined with wool. The inner parts had been rolled and weren't too waterlogged, but even hanging near the fire it wouldn't dry very fast. I left my linen chemise on, wrapped up in the cloak, and started a small fire while waiting for the fish. Good thing my family was wealthy enough for me to own deerskin pants. They were thinner than most leather and would dry faster.

The last bits of hard cheese and jerky were salvageable. I often soaked them before eating anyway.

My first catch on the line was small, but I couldn't afford to be choosy. The second was large enough to make a difference.

I needed to find a safe place to settle for a week or so to replenish a store of jerky. It was that or hope to find a small village in Wendal that didn't know about me. The thought of bread and fresh cheese had me sighing with longing.

Dusk had long since draped itself around the fire. The smoke would now be less noticeable, and my chemise was only damp in patches. Sleeping in it was not a comforting thought. Luckily, I had other options.

Of course, I wasn't counting on the dragon.

Chapter 4

When the baby dragon flew into my camp, he managed an impressive snort that included a tiny flame. I'd not have seen it had he not been right in front of my face in the dark.

"Watch it there, Sparky. Scorching fire like that could cause a girl an uneven sunburn, and who would marry me then?"

The little round ball of scales zipped over to my fire and settled himself down to pick at the bones from the fish.

"Nice of you to join me. Did your friend make it?" Looking much like a large bird, he fluffed himself in the ashes, rolling around and basking in the heat.

Had I not been concentrating so much on the little dragon, I might have noticed the larger one swooping in. Then again, she glided almost silently to the tops of the trees and half changed to human on her way down, a feat I was not used to worrying about.

I hated fighting in my underwear, but my dagger was out, and the cloak dropped in an instant. I was in a defensive position without thinking about it. The only real question was whether I was supposed to defend Spark or if he was supposed to defend me, given that this was one of his kind, not mine.

"Greetings. I am Lindis of Wendal." Her voice was a rumble, a sultry kind of thunder. "The fireling tells me you saved him."

She was either unaware of my knife or completely unconcerned. Let's see. I had just seen a human body form underneath two giant wings. She had sported large clawed hands and feet until she landed.

With a sigh, I sheathed the dagger back in my boot. Dragons probably had night vision, and even if she had seen the knife, it no doubt looked like a mosquito swatter to her. Scaled boots now covered what had been talons, and her hands were perfect human digits rather than lethal weapons. Black eyes stared out from a face not much older than my own twenty years. She was clothed in a sleeveless scaled tunic and pants.

"Saved him?" I shook my head. "No, I just picked him up on the way through."

"He mentioned your food sources were..." She paused, her head tilting. "Lacking?"

"That's not quite it. Closer to 'though you were on starvation rations you shared.'"

"I only had a few bits of jerky left that he was likely to eat." I gestured with my chin. "If I'd known he intended to stop in tonight, I would have saved him some fish."

She shrugged. "He found the remains of the fish guts, and those toasted bones are good for him, although he would have preferred them raw."

"Yes, well, I thought he planned to stay with—" Now I paused. "The forest was safer for him, especially with two miscreants on my trail."

"What happened to the poachers?"

"I left them behind." I waved to the river. "Swam away, and they were not inclined to follow."

"They have crimes to answer for. Can you spare a few moments of your time to help us locate them?" Her fists clenched, and she didn't bother to relax when she pointed at Spark. "He would be in your debt a second time, as would Falk. Both are already your allies, but it never hurts to seal a bargain officially."

"Falk?"

"The one you carried away. He attempted to stop the murderous thieves before your arrival, but failed."

Dismay filled me even though I had suspected the crime. "Murderous? They killed the dragon's mother, then?"

"Nothing short of death would cause a mother dragonkin to leave her egg, especially during a hatching."

"When the one mentioned dragonsbane I hoped—" At her indrawn breath I stopped speaking.

"Did you see it? There are legends of such, but it has been eons since anyone has found a way to grow it."

I shook my head. "No, I'd never even heard of it, but one of them yelled about it when they spotted Spark, the fireling."

One eyebrow quirked at my having given the dragonkin a name, but she didn't argue. "This is precisely the kind of detail we require. Will you come with me? Falk will search you out in any case. You may as well accept his thanks in person."

"I'm glad he made it. I left him in a bad situation, but it wasn't possible for me to carry him further. Please give him my regards. I'll happily answer your questions, but I'm afraid I must decline your invitation. I've places I need to go."

She stared at me, more of a glare than anything else. "There would be food and a dry bed. Supplies to get you to your destination."

While I had just been contemplating my lack of supplies, gullibility and trust were not part of my character. "I'm sorry. I must decline."

"You planned to stay here for the night, yes?"

I nodded. Now that she had found me, my plans had changed, although moving wasn't likely to do me much good. The little fireling had located me easily, and if it could trace me, she could probably do so as well. Perhaps escaping to Wendal had not been the best of ideas. The politics might be different here, and no one here owed anyone in Anton, but that didn't mean it was safe.

"Then one night elsewhere will not set you back. I'll take you to your destination tomorrow morning. I travel quickly so it will save you considerable time."

Checkmate. It was run and try to hide or give in gracefully. I did neither. I returned her stare, wondering if she would force me to go.

Chapter 5

In the end, Lindis turned dragon and wasted hot air drying my cloak, pants and tunic. Spark joined in, blowing on one corner for all he was worth, which amounted to him belching a miniscule ball of fire. Had the cloak not been wet, he might have set it on fire. He, however, strutted proudly, impressed with the flame he produced, quite possibly the best he had managed thus far.

"You can ride. Or I can carry you," Lindis informed me.

I assumed she meant using her claws, with me dangling like prey. "I'll ride, thanks." Escaping would be possible if I chose to dive to my death. Maybe we'd take off over the river, and I could jump in.

Impossibly tired, I gathered my things and climbed aboard. Spark settled on my shoulder, peeping in my ear, full of stories that, without a translator, were nothing more than noise. He fluttered up and down, bouncing like an excited child, getting bowled over backwards by an errant breeze when Lindis banked sharply.

Chattering like a squirrel, he righted himself and was on my shoulder again by the time I hopped off.

Lindis changed to fully human.

A pretty lady with long dark braids about my age held a crystal high, illuminating the clearing where we had landed. Next to her, a burly individual waited protectively. His eyes reflected a luminous yellow from the light. Black and dark gray hair mixed with lighter streaks as though his head was designed to blend into the forest shadows.

My legs were almost steady when the man I had rescued was suddenly leaning against a tree and close enough to touch if I reached out.

His face was only lightly bruised now, and his arm had somehow healed enough that he crossed both arms across his broad chest without a problem. His gold and white hair was no longer caked with blood. Craggy bones made his face almost delicate if you discounted watchful eyes that trapped me with their intensity.

"I promised her supplies for travel in exchange for information," Lindis said to no one in particular.

"She can have that without the asking. And with it my thanks, Lady."

The injured man's nod was as courtly a bow as I'd ever seen, even though he didn't bother to bend at the waist.

They all stared at me. I watched them back, not about to start babbling just because I was surrounded.

Finally the woman holding the glowing crystal without benefit of a lantern to house it said, "I'm Zoe, formerly of Birk, house of cloth and metal. This is my husband, Derrick. You've met Lindis, assuming she was polite enough to introduce herself before carting you here." Lindis flashed a threatening snarl her way, but Zoe ignored it. "And of course, you have met Falk, although I dare say there was no time for proper introductions."

"Drissa." They could add any flourishes with their imagination. Let them guess that I was the niece of a noble-wannabe playing games in Anton in an attempt to raise himself far above his station.

If they recognized the name from any far-reaching rumors, no one reacted.

Derrick inclined his head and grinned. Zoe smiled and Falk nodded.

Spark chirped in my ear.

"The little one is hungry again," Lindis said. "That is as good a place to start as any."

Derrick and Zoe led the way to a stone cottage flanked by a small stream. There was a large cellar set into a hillside and trees enough to keep the structures fairly well hidden. Lindis stayed on my right, leaving Falk behind us.

Instead of following, he volunteered, "I'll bring supplies."

Lindis nodded without turning so I kept walking.

The inside of the cottage was small, but warm and homey.

It soon smelled of grilling meat, onions, bread and cheese. Before the cooking was even close to done, I was nearly asleep, propped in a chair with my back to one wall.

Zoe left the kitchen to whisper in my ear. She offered clean clothes, which I accepted, along with a shower. To my delight, the clothing was styled like my own, rather than a skirt or dress.

Of course, both Zoe and Lindis wore pants, assuming the decorative scales Lindis sported were such. The dragon's attire seemed to be more a part of her than regular leathers, but other than an odd sheen, the scales were barely visible, making them suitable pants—if a bit tighter than I would wear.

Zoe was slim like me, but she was two or three inches taller. Her clothes fit well once I tacked the leathers up on either side. The borrowed clothes were made of goatskin, a mix of white and black mismatched hides. No one in Anton would wear such a mix to court, but not only would they serve as camouflage in the shadows of the forest, they were lovely and as soft as my deerskin. Perhaps I could purchase them from Zoe.

By the time I was clean, warm tea waited and Falk had returned. He handed me a pack that was half the size of the one I already carried. I set it inside mine. "My thanks." I hesitated. It was only right I should offer payment, but Falk's steady stare warned against it.

"Traveling far?" His melodic baritone echoed off the walls even though he had not spoken loudly.

I nodded. "Hopefully."

A small smile tilted his lips upward, but most of his amusement was reflected in eyes flecked with beautiful browns and reds. "There should be enough in the pack for more than a week for a small bit like yourself. You're welcome to it and more should you need it. The forest knows my name if you ever have a request."

"I did no more than..." To claim any stranger would have helped as I had was pushing even the bounds of polite chatter. I smiled. "Than Spark demanded. He refused to leave you, attempting to cart you off by dragging you by one finger. It did not look as though he could quite manage it on his own."

Falk crossed his arms. For such a lanky individual, his chest and shoulders were very broad. His shirt was a coarse linen rather than the material he had worn before, which had been a soft, almost downy silk. When he shifted positions, his strong muscles were still evident. "Lindis claims the fireling said you carried me, but when they found me I was not hawk. I do not remember turning one way or the other. Which was it?"

Turning hawk. I let the phrase sit across my tired brain for a moment or two. No wonder he had strong shoulders. Finally I said, "No, you weren't hawk. It would have been far easier if you had been. As it was, I tripped over a log, dropped you into a pile of leaves, and sadly, left you for dead." I shook my head apologetically. "Spark may have distracted the miscreants, but I was too busy running to save my own hide." I spread my hands. "So you see, you owe me nothing really, although I might be responsible for a bruise or two."

Lindis added her two pence. "You carried him far enough. Spark, as you call him, was not required to risk himself further. If they had dragonsbane as you claim, it would have been the end of him."

"Dragonsbane? What's that?" Zoe's head swiveled from the table where she was piling food.

No one waited to be served, so I quickly heaped my plate high with the rest of them.

Lindis helped herself from a plate of meat that was quite rare, but she must have eaten already because her plate wasn't nearly so full as Derrick's.

Falk chose the fully cooked meat. Spark accepted a large chunk of meat from Lindis while she explained. "Dragonsbane was used against us in the war. It's a mage magic, sometimes a plant, sometimes a magic encased in a crystal. It's used in an attempt to control or thwart dragons. The weapon came about late in the war when negotiations were already in the works for peace. If it still exists, it stayed on your side of the border after the veil was raised that cut Wendal off from the other territories."

Zoe muttered what might have been a curse. Still chewing, she approached the fireplace mantle and extracted a book.

I blinked. There had been only stones there before.

She returned to the table, flipping pages. "Dragonsbane? Plant?" She scowled, pacing back to the fireplace to extract a second book. She looked up at Lindis. "The gryphon used a magical element in the ring that kept you from being able to turn into your dragon form. Could the secret ingredient in the spelled ring have been dragonsbane? The grimoire never directly named all the requirements."

This time when Zoe replaced the volume and selected another, I saw the heavy tome shimmer into form. An illusion. Zoe was a mage.

It was time for me to part with what information I had to offer and leave. "I wish I could help, but nothing I witnessed could possibly be of any use. Spark's mother was already gone, dragged away. Spark was busy eating eggshells when one of the men shouted and decided to return to the ravine. Before I could take my leave, Spark pointed out Falk."

"And you carried me away."

I shrugged and winced, but not from the memory. Carrying a pack for weeks was bad enough, but toting Falk about for a mile had left my shoulders sore. He looked to be only a few inches shy of six feet tall to my five-four, and he had been excruciatingly heavy. "Honestly, if Spark hadn't given me a head start by distracting the two men who came back, we'd never have made it. As it was, once they were on my trail, they were splitting their time between following me and hunting for Spark. They'd have closed in easily otherwise."

"Did you hear them talk of their plans?"

"No, not a word." I thought hard, searching my memory. "Mostly they argued over whether Spark was a dragon or a bird and whether to use the dragonsbane. One guy seemed anxious to use it, while the other warned against it, almost as though it might only be good for a single use. Or blow in the wrong direction. But I don't know what he meant or how they intended to use it. I'm not a mage. I studied a few tricks growing up, but we all tried our hand at some basic magics. I never learned more than how to start a fire when necessary and light lanterns." I'd been too busy taking other lessons from Grandmother to get into trouble with mage magic.

Zoe nodded and smiled at me. Being from Birk, she understood. The others were obviously from Wendal, and it was said that Wendal's magic was different from that of the four kingdoms because of the barrier that had been erected at the border. On our side, every child played with magic, at least until we were caught or burned our own fingers enough times to wise up.

"Any spell will wear out," Zoe said. "The power has to be renewed, and if what they are using is plant based, it could burn up entirely or be good for one use only." She turned to Lindis. "You said the dragonkin aren't full dragons like you. It would take less of this dragonsbane then, right?"

My head swiveled to Lindis. "Wait. What? Not a full dragon?"

Lindis nodded once. "The kin are not shifters. They are a smaller species of dragon, the animal version only. They grow to about the size of a wolf. That is possibly the reason the poachers mistook Spark for a bird. A true dragon is far larger at birth than the fireling you saved."

I glanced down at Spark. He had managed to steal another steak from Lindis. He was content to eat wherever the food landed, unlike the rest of us sitting in chairs. "How did he find me after we were separated?"

Lindis smiled. "Once he was convinced the poachers weren't coming back for Falk, he flew after you. He said the men gave up on you shortly after you dove in the water. He followed you downstream until you emerged. Then he went back to Falk, but we had found him by then, and were bringing him here."

"You speak to Spark?"

"He's dragon. I'm dragon."

"But you're in human form."

"Forms do not matter. He knows I am dragon."

"Can he speak to Falk?"

Lindis raised an amused brow. "Not really. Although he does refer to him as a hawk, regardless of his form."

"The size of a wolf," I said. "You are much larger than that when you're dragon."

"Of course. More than double."

Zoe put in, "Large war horse, but broader."

I was too tired to connect that with my original thought. My eyes nearly crossed with the effort it took to keep them open.

Lindis stood. "I'll be by in the morn. Falk?"

He was also standing, a motion I had missed. He strode to the door, almost gliding, even though no wings were in evidence. "I'd be happy to escort you, should you require a guide in Wendal," he told me, pausing at the front door.

"I'll be fine."

He stared at me as though he intended to say something more, but then changed his mind. In one blink, he was gone. The party was over.

Zoe offered me a pallet of blankets and furs. Derrick left just after Lindis and Falk for what Zoe said was a "perimeter check." She hesitated and then added, "It's obvious you are not from Wendal. Derrick is a wolf. So if he goes furry on us, it isn't him you need to fear. For that matter, any wolf you see near here is part of his pack."

"And you?"

"Me what?"

"You're a mage. But do you get furry? Or feathery? Or scaled?"

Zoe laughed. "Oh, no. I'm from Birk. Human. Boring. And barely more than half a mage by official training. I have learned to fill in the blanks with things the university at Gorgon never taught." She dimmed the crystals, leaving us in near darkness.

Spark startled me by hopping into my lap. He chirped and preened his scales.

I snuggled under the blankets.

When the wolf returned, silent as he was, I woke enough to reach for my dagger before remembering. His yellow eyes blinked at me once in the dark.

Something about his size bothered me, but sleep called too loudly for me to chase the thought.

Spark the dragonkin was a comforting little ball of warmth next to me. If he or anything else snored or threatened, I was too exhausted to notice.

Chapter 6

Derrick was cracking eggs over a hot skillet in the morning when I woke. Zoe was deep in a book, muttering and taking notes. I took care of morning rituals and offered to help in the kitchen.

I wondered if I should move my pack from the chair where I had placed it the night before, but no one else seemed to care about it, so there it remained while I set plates and forks on the table.

There was warm goat's milk, a treat Zoe was already drinking. I helped myself and offered a bowl of it to Spark. He seemed well pleased with it and half a dozen raw eggs. His eating habits had caused a growth spurt. Instead of the duckling-sized dragonkin that had hatched, he was the size of a full grown duck with a very long neck and a tail that wrapped all the way around his large feet.

"He'll eat eggs cooked or not," Derrick informed me. "He'll eat most anything if you want the truth, and as often as he can, too." He set down a plate of scrambled eggs. There was already a large pile of smoked meat, either a ham or bacon, waiting on the table.

"Should have cooked up some beets or potatoes," Zoe murmured, digging in, but still reading.

"Forgot to bring them." From the grin on Derrick's face, he probably 'forgot' on purpose. He went back to the wood stove and retrieved a skillet piled high with steaming potatoes, onions and beets.

Zoe rolled her eyes at him, finally setting the book aside.

Their light banter reminded me of life before we moved to Uncle Ralph's castle. Derrick was not unlike my father—protective, competent and watchful, but relaxed and fun too.

Before my mood could turn maudlin over the way things should have been, Lindis and Falk showed up with a new person trailing in behind them.

Zoe sat up straighter, and her lip curled. "Cousin Lonnie. You're back."

He spread his arms as though waiting for a hug. "Of course! Missed me, didn't you?" He chuckled, brandishing one hand over his heart, displaying a garish display of sparkling rings on each of his fingers. Unlike the rest of us, he was fully decked out for court in bright woolen pants with a tunic trimmed with braids of silver and gold.

"I do hope no one is attempting to apprehend you this time," was Zoe's response to his pomp.

Lonnie smoothed one hand over his wild hair, but it sprang right back up. Instead of keeping it tied back, the snow-white strands floated as though he had rubbed his head against a wall to generate enough static to keep it airborne.

"I brought you the book you wanted!" he announced. There was a puff of smoke, a flash, and then he was hopping about, slapping at sudden flames that were eagerly devouring a thick, leather bound book.

Zoe muttered a single word, and the fire extinguished itself. "I'll take it before you burn it. Most books are protected against idiots such as yourself, but I see you managed to negate those spells." She snagged the tome before Cousin Lonnie could even close his mouth.

Everyone else ignored the exchange in favor of eating. Out of instinct, I found that the straps to my pack were gripped in my left hand in preparation for a quick exit out the back door. I set it back near my feet and helped myself to food.

Lonnie grabbed a chair and began eating as well. He managed to eat and babble about spending the night with the other wolves, remarking about someone named Star being thrilled to see him.

Derrick's growl was low enough that it was more vibration than sound, but Zoe must have heard it too because she said, "Your sister can handle herself and twenty Lonnies if need be."

The growl reminded me of the wolf last night. I stopped chewing and stared at Derrick. He was tall, probably just over six feet in his human form. His wolf had been huge, much larger than a dog, but not as large as a horse. A small pony maybe.

He noticed me staring and stopped his own chewing. "I'll not hurt you," he said.

"You aren't that big," I replied, thinking of the drag marks in the dragon's ravine.

Derrick's eyebrows shot up, and Falk didn't bother to stifle a snort. Now everyone was looking at me.

Lindis said, "It isn't wise to challenge a wolf in his own house. Whether you think you can take him down or not."

I blinked. "Oh. That isn't what I meant. I was thinking of the scuffle where I found Spark. There were bushes half torn out and more damage than would have been caused by a single dragon the size of one wolf."

"From the fight?" Lindis looked at Falk for confirmation.

He scowled. "I came late to it. I can't even remember if I was hit or when. There was the oddest pop in my brain when I attacked. I dove as bird, but she claims she carried me out as human."

"Does dragonsbane work on hawks?" I asked.

Lindis tossed another piece of meat to Spark. He plucked it from the air. "There is nothing in my memory banks other than what I told you already. We are similar to hawks in some aspects. It's possible."

"Whatever was dragged out of that ravine was larger than a wolf. Or there were two of them." The bushes had leaned and been broken down in more than one direction. "What of Spark's father?"

We all looked at the happy little dragon. He belched a small flame, got reprimanded by Lindis for his lack of control, and then the two of them stared at one another.

After she broke the stare, she said, "Much dragonkin lore is passed on through the mother even before hatching; it works the same way with us. He is born with a history and full instincts for survival. He could hear through the shell, especially as his hatching neared. He remembers his father as coming and going and only occasionally carrying him around. He remembers his parents' panic, but after some initial flaming and flight, his mother sat on him until she wasn't there anymore. He also remembers the challenge of a hawk war cry."

She frowned. "It's quite possible the dragonkin parents sensed the poachers, flew in different directions and circled back to fight. That is a common dragon defense, but that would mean the poachers captured two dragons." Steam puffed out of her ears.

Lonnie broke in. "Why hasn't anyone introduced me to this fine lady? I swear, Zoe. You leave the court, and you forget all your manners." He stood and made a courtly bow.

I frowned. This hardly seemed the time or the place.

Zoe's hand on my arm indicated I did not have to stand and return the bow. It would have been a waste of time in any case because Lonnie was busy spouting titles and accomplishments. I heard, "Esteemed Wizard of Birk" and the son of some lineage or other and something about being nearly kin to Prince Kal, firstborn of Birk.

At the mention of the prince, his eyes darted to Lindis.

She hissed at him.

He stumbled over more words mentioning how he was a mentor and not really a relative of the prince and couldn't be held accountable for mischief when Prince Kal demanded he call a dragon to court. When his stutters finally plowed to a stop, he sucked in much needed air and blinked at me, waiting.

"Drissa."

Everyone appeared to be holding their breath in anticipation of more. I frowned and tried to be polite. "Your acquaintance will likely be..." I couldn't force the standard, "a boon" after the mess he had just presented, "of value to those far and wide." Let someone else find him valuable.

"Drissa! What a lovely name! Means 'of the oaks,' right? Then, you must—" He stopped, his mouth gaping open for too scant a moment. "Hey, you're not the Drissa from Anton, are you? The one who was kidnapped right before the marriage mart for Prince Irwin?" His eyes widened, but his mouth continued flapping. "Everyone announced their daughters last month. Drissa was said to be a prime choice because her uncle promised a solution to Irwin's nearly forced dragon alliance last year—said Drissa came with a dowry that would ensure that no dragon would ever be able to come and claim revenge for the kidnapping of the dragon."

I was halfway through the kitchen, headed for the back exit before the wolf stood. He'd easily have nabbed me in a single bound, but Lonnie saved me.

"Hey, if it's her, I get the reward!" He threw something and screamed an unintelligible word. Whatever he tossed hit Derrick instead of me. The force of it pushed Derrick sideways into the stove.

As my feet cleared the door I heard Zoe scream, "YOU BLOOMING IDIOT! Lonnie, I swear I am going to kill you one day!"

I ran headlong without looking back.

Chapter 7

My steady stride was easier this time mostly because I was well-fed and rested. There was also no point in wasting time worrying about being caught. What chance did I have? The wolf could smell me out, especially in his territory. The hawk and dragons could fly overhead, and the dragon could pluck me up at will.

Never one to give up easily, I took evasive actions, circling around and under thick trees, running to the side and back, always heading west. The border of Wendal and Birk was east. Anton was east and north—all avoidable.

The supplies Falk had provided were heavy. It took me a while to get my pack situated comfortably across my shoulders given that they were still sore, and I was jogging steadily.

Lindis and her friends had promised I could go free. Maybe they wouldn't give chase.

There was still Lonnie. He had certainly seemed interested in curtailing my freedom. Reward? What could he possibly be blathering about? Uncle Ralph would never offer a reward for me, and he had planned to announce impending nuptials, not inform us that I was in the running as a possible choice. Maybe once I had disappeared, Uncle claimed I had been kidnapped, and the king had changed the announcement from "impending nuptials" to "will select from random marriage mart material."

A branch smacked into my head because I wasn't paying close enough attention to my path. I apologized to it and continued on.

Because of her gift, Grandmother was the best and sneakiest spy in the business. She had heard something that gave her reason to believe Uncle Ralph had the deal sealed. How could he possibly have convinced Prince Irwin or the king that I was the perfect match? We had assumed my heritage had been the carrot, but what if it was something else, this thing Lonnie hinted at that would keep dragons from extracting revenge?

My knowledge of court intrigue was sadly lacking. I had a vague memory of Prince Irwin being temporarily betrothed to a dragon from Wendal, but details had been wildly exaggerated. Lonnie had implied that the dragon had been snatched in a political deal, but how did one coerce a war-horse sized fire-breathing dragon to do something against its will? And if you did and the deal fell apart, what possible dowry could ensure against dragon revenge?

My feet stopped, and I gasped.   Lindis and Zoe had been very concerned about dragonsbane being used in some spell or other.

"No way. Uncle isn't a mage. He's too cheap to even hire one on a regular basis. He can't have found out about dragonsbane. And even if he did, he wouldn't know how to use it in a spell to coerce a dragon or kidnap one or stop one." But if there was a way to make money, Uncle Ralph could smell it miles away.

A chirp from behind me announced Spark's arrival. He landed on my pack with an enthusiastic thump.

"Ooof." The baggage was already heavy enough. "You're putting on weight, Spark." And if he had found me, the others were, no doubt, close behind.

Time to lose and discourage them.

I studied the trees more closely as I hurried along. I didn't want to pick an area where my disappearance would be too noticeable. Any copse with a few younger oaks, but with enough full grown trees for shelter would do.

Despite the fact that I had explored much of Anton while growing up, I had not put down roots often enough to be quick about it. Father's weekly hunting trips ensured I had some regular practice, but most of my learning was saved for outings with Grandmother. Even so, much of my training had taken place near the castle.

I stopped, secured my pack between my feet where it would be encased in the trunk and concentrated. To my surprise, forming roots in Wendal was easier than in Anton. The soil was rich and full of nutrients. Being only a quarter dryad to my grandmother's full, I had never excelled at photosynthesis, but changing to a hearty red oak was something I had achieved by age five.

I had dreaded the practice times when Grandmother insisted I drink from the earth because anywhere near the castle the water was often tainted from the many villages. Here, the damp soil tasted fresh, and since I was thirsty, I drank my fill of clean water.

Grandmother was full dryad. Changing to tree at least once a month was mandatory for her survival. For me, it had been more of a chore than anything. I loved the forest, but rarely bothered to join it.

This time, becoming tree felt magnificent as I stretched to the sky and drank in the late spring sunlight. My fingers reached for the beams of energy, and the hair on my arms bristled into leaves. The smooth grain of wood was an old friend, a physical exercise I hadn't known I missed until now. Maybe this is what it felt like for hawks when they shifted and flew. What was it like to leave the boundaries of earth and own the sky?

My toes wiggled in the dirt with great satisfaction. I had forgotten the subtle whispers of the other trees. In human form, I spared little more than a kind word here and there. But I was one of them and as such, the forest greeted me happily, buzzing with healthy plant hormones and a song of a thousand trees muttering their contentment.

I sighed, relaxing for the first time in a month.

Spark didn't seem to notice my transformation. He merely settled on a branch in full sunlight and began to snooze.

Not a bad idea, not a bad one at all. I whispered of my interest in dragons and wolves to the nearby trees, then let the gentle wind lull me into a doze.

I had spent more than one night as a tree at Grandmother's insistence, but it had been a wary slumber with more than a touch of teenage boredom. Even now, I did not sleep deep enough to dream, but there were flitting images of birds, fluttering leaves and forest songs that were not entirely my own thoughts.

The other trees didn't warn me specifically about the wolf because they accepted him as a part of the forest, just like the passing squirrels and rabbits. They remembered my interest though.

He comes.

In this form, even with nothing to hide, I tensed. I reminded myself that my trunk and branches were merely another tree. Well, unless you counted the fact that Spark the dragonkin was sitting on me.

He chirped a happy hello when the wolf padded nearby and promptly flew down to squawk a louder greeting. Luckily, he was learning control. He fluttered and bobbed his tail with barely any sparks escaping.

The wolf sat back on his haunches and growled a greeting. He wisely kept his nose far from Spark's happy advances.

To my surprise, the wolf changed his head and shoulders to human. He was as furry as he had been the moment before except for his face. "Where did she go?" he asked. "The trail ends here."

Lindis hadn't said the wolf could speak dragon. I held my breath, not even daring to use up carbon dioxide.

Spark gave his version of a triumphant roar, which sounded a lot like crunching gravel, and flew to my shoulder.

I waited, but the wolf apparently didn't understand.

When the hawk landed, he did as Lindis had done, changing on the way down. The feathers shortened, becoming the leathers I had wondered about; a mottled mix of whites, browns and golds, clothing him from his head to his feet. This time, he wore a sheath across his back and shoulders. The leather band holding it on stretched as he changed, leaving the short sword comfortably within reach should he need it.

The wolf straightened to full man, his fur knitting itself into sleek trousers.

"You stopped tracking," Falk said.

"The scent ends here."

Falk shook his head. "She isn't ahead or behind. I circled twice."

"Perhaps we should have started earlier and followed closer," Derrick mused. "But I don't generally lose my prey."

Falk's head swiveled fast. "She isn't prey."

Derrick shrugged. "It was a comparison. I have trouble tracking your kind, but unless it flies, it usually isn't a problem."

Falk stared up past the overhead canopy. "She did not take to the air. Although that would make her even more interesting."

Derrick grinned. "She is a beauty."

"She is strong."

"And on the run." Derrick sniffed deeply. "Her scent isn't gone exactly. It just doesn't go anywhere from here."

"Is she shifter then?" Falk asked.

"Not that I can tell. She smells human with an earthy scent. I was surprised when Lonnie guessed she was from Anton because she smells more of the forest, like moss and fresh greenery. I'd have bet she spent a lot of time in the woods." His face changed to half a muzzle. Without hesitation, he sniffed the base of me.

When he spoke again, his voice was deeper and full of growl. "She was more difficult to track than a normal human. Her false trails where she circled trees nearly hid her scent. Now it is completely gone. There is nothing but trees and no scent of her at all."

Well, he had it mostly right.

"She kept her end of the bargain," Falk sighed. "She was free to go in any case."

Derrick nodded, his face changing to full human again. "It's not safe for one like her traveling alone in Wendal."

Falk agreed. "It doesn't sound like it was safe for her in Anton either."

Both men stared at me, hard. It wasn't until Spark darted after a rabbit that I realized they were watching the dragon, not the tree. Spark's preoccupation with food saved me from any real threat of discovery.

Derrick grunted and loped off to the right. A check with the other trees informed me that he had curled under a maple a few yards off.

Falk changed, flapped onto one of my branches and sat, contemplating the area.

He hopped to a couple of nearby trees. After inspecting them and the surrounding areas, he glided down to the low bushes nearby. He even pecked at the leaves behind a large boulder.

When Spark finished his rabbit and flew back onto one of my branches, Falk clicked at him and then launched himself from the ground, adding his own weight to the branch.

Spark twittered back quietly, as he preened and washed up.

It surprised me to realize my sense of animal speak was stronger as a tree. I didn't understand any words, but the tone of the exchange was one of ease. Neither of them likely understood exactly what was said, but they seemed to convey a sense of welcome and calm.

Falk scooted in close to my main trunk, and I worried he might peck me with his beak, but he seemed to be smelling me, searching for bits of essence that made up the heart of the tree. His head cocked one way and then the other. He tucked his head nearly between his feet, studying the branch where he sat.

Finally he straightened and clicked again, almost a happy chuckle. Spark gave a questioning chirp, but Falk didn't answer. Instead, he danced back and forth on the branch, testing its mettle or perhaps...It felt as though he had run a gentle hand down my arm.

He twittered softly, hopped to a higher branch, and glided across me again, like light fingertips plucking the wood ever so gently. My stomach fluttered as the delicate scrape of his claws caressed me, creating an odd resonance across my bark.

Did hawks normally stroke tree branches? His talons hugged the wood, almost cradling that part of me. He used his wings for balance, leaving no gouges or injuries upon my person.

After another light caress or two, he hopped back down to the first branch, inspected the trunk again and then settled in close to it. He tucked his head into his chest reminding me of Spark, who had already curled into himself.

The two of them roosted quite comfortably in my arms.

As darkness fell, Falk crooned just the tiniest bit, as if reassuring anyone nearby that he was keeping watch.

I had forgotten about the wolf until that moment, but Falk's quiet singing had me waving my leaves in question at the other trees.

Derrick had moved off very quietly as dusk set. That made sense. He had a wife at home, territory to protect, and no doubt, better things to do than follow a stranger through the woods.

But why had Falk stayed?

Well, I guess the bird had to sleep somewhere.

I guess I did too.

Chapter 8

I awoke starved. My leaves fluttered every which way trying to catch the sun, but it hadn't quite risen over the horizon. Even so, if the past was any indication, it would be a long day of hungry if I had to rely on photosynthesis. Then again, I'd never been quite this hungry as a tree either.

Falk was already awake. He squawked a greeting, flexed his claws and launched into the air.

He was truly beautiful, his wings beating strong and fast, taking him to soaring heights in less than a minute. Maybe I appreciated him more because I was a tree, a part of his world at the moment. That was probably the reason my breath caught as I watched him fly away.

Spark fluttered off to look for rabbits while I twittered my leaves, waiting for sunlight. Falk circled twice, but each time he was higher in the sky. Hawk eyes were keen. I'd have to wait until I didn't see him at all and even then there was risk. That bird knew the forest much more intimately than I and considering my quarter-dryad heritage that was a sad thing.

The sun finally sparkled and dressed the morning in pink and orange. My leaves greedily reached for the first weak rays. Photosynthesizing was like having a giant meal spread before you—and you were allowed to eat one pea sized bite at a time, but only after chewing it thoroughly.

I checked with the other trees, whispering my question with the rustling of my leaves.

There were no wolves nearby. Plenty of birds, two owls and one hawk. None were particularly close, and if the birds weren't in the air, they couldn't see me. Well, probably not.

I pulled up roots and changed, sighing back into my human form. Somewhat like the shifters, I didn't have to worry about clothing. Bark covered my clothes, and wood grew around the packs and other things I carried so long as I controlled my form properly.

First things first. I opened the pack Falk had given me and found cheese and bread. The jerky could wait until later and would last longer in any case. I wasn't thirsty in the least, so while the extra waterskin he had enclosed was a bonus, I didn't require it at the moment.

The bread wasn't even hard yet, and the cheese was made from goat's milk, still soft and crumbly. I hoped he had packed harder cheeses below.

While I chewed, I inspected the rest of the gifted goods, surprised to see a note secured with rough hemp string around a crystal.

The handwriting on the rough paper was in small, cramped letters. In case I had forgotten how to command light from a crystal, there were careful instructions for tying myself to the crystal and setting it properly. There was one set of instructions for creating light and another for setting the thing off in an explosion. Well. What a thoughtful gift. Zoe had signed her name and "be well" at the end.

It occurred to me that she could use the crystal to trace me, and for a moment, I considered leaving it behind. Spark darted between the note and my eyeballs, a reminder that if the group of shifters and mages really wanted to find me, they probably could anyway.

I memorized the note, and set the crystal for instant use upon command as instructed. It was small enough to tuck in my pocket where it would be readily available.

The rest of the pack contained various foodstuffs including more soft cheese, dried as well as fresh bread, and plenty of jerky.

In the very bottom of the pack, another surprise waited. Nestled in deerskin I found two soft feathers, one white and one gold, tied together with a leather braid. As soon as I picked up the feather, I noticed the leather wrapping them was etched with the strokes from a delicate knife—or claw. Upon study, it was apparent that the words and symbols were a map of Wendal.

Well. This was a generous gift.

The map was not signed, but the feathers had me marveling at Falk's kindness. Of course, he had included the map before he knew I was on the run. Would he have been so eager to repay my kindness had he known I was a fugitive? And that my very own uncle might be involved in trading dragonsbane spells to ensure my marriage?

Not that I could ever be certain what Uncle was involved in, but Falk might not have been so generous had he known my relatives were of such questionable ilk.

Falk could probably trace me through the feathers. I glanced skyward, tensing at the thought of having to outrun him. If last night was any indication, he hadn't really lost track of me. But how had he guessed my dryad side? Was it just that he knew the forest so well he had sensed something different about my tree form?

Grandmother had trained me well. Not a bit of my face ever remained, although it was easy enough to leave an expression across the bark if I chose. I knew how to harden every bit of me so that nothing short of a sharp blade could hurt me, but it was equally easy to flop a branch about so that it couldn't be snapped off.

The quills of Falk's feathers were hollow and strong, but the rest of the feather was quite delicate. If I stored them in a pocket they would surely be crushed. I looped the leather braid around my neck and tucked the feathers under my tunic. They'd be safe there.

Finished with my breakfast, I packed up and checked out the deerskin map. I needed to compare it to the one Grandmother had supplied, but at the moment, the best direction was still west. Sooner or later, I had to find a suitable village or town where I could blend in.

I hadn't found any settlements thus far in Wendal. There had been isolated homes much like Derrick's cottage, but it was safer to avoid those. A single homestead would easily remember each visitor and could pass along such information to the next traveler.

With Lonnie announcing me to the entire room, further travel seemed prudent. Of course, he had only heard of me because he'd been back to Birk. How many others here could know? And how many others would he tell?

I sighed and started walking.

Spark was good company. He was not, however, much for sharing his food. He caught no less than four rabbits in the morning. He'd stay behind briefly to eat, and then he'd land on my pack for a nap.

"You're part pig," I told him. "At least you take baths regularly." What he didn't lick off his person he burned off with his enthusiastic grooming. The fire that smoldered in his stomach popped and sizzled as he snoozed. Every now and then a puff of smoke drifted from his nostrils.

When I stopped for lunch, he finally consented to share the skinned and neatly dissected back parts of his sixth rabbit. "I hadn't planned on building a fire." But I wasn't going to eat the thing raw. I gathered kindling.

Helpfully, he zoomed over and belched out a flame. There was enough force behind it that the kindling scattered, but not enough fire to actually light it.

I scooted the pieces back into place and lit the fire myself. I scratched his neck scales. "You might come in handy yet, but you'll have to grow some."

He butted his head against my hand so I obliged with another scritch. "Hmm. Looks like a bump here." I inspected his neck and found no less than four protrusions under the scales. "Ah. Horns coming in? Itches?"

He burbled or purred and puffed smoke out.

As soon as I extracted my grilled rabbit from the flames, he hopped into the fire and rolled onto his back, letting the bits of hot wood scratch his back.

I ate and withdrew the map Grandmother had given me to compare with Falk's gift.

My original version was sadly lacking. One mountain range to the south was marked as Griffin territory. Falk's map agreed, but spelled it "Gryphon" and the territories were smaller. Only on the highest, rockiest peaks were Gryphon territories noted on his map.

Below the peaks, little stick trees decorated the mountain ranges.

According to the map, dwarfs and gnomes lived in at least one of the ranges. Falk had marked two large territories with a dragon symbol, and one had the word "Lindis" under the dragon flame. There were bear and cat drawings seemingly at random, but neither of those species were pack animals. Spiked tails labeled "dragonkin" indicated that the kin lived in close-knit territories more often than not.

There were no less than three large territories marked for hawks and falcons. Derrick's glen was plainly marked also.

Falk's name was etched in two different places. Wouldn't you know one was directly west of Derrick's glen where I was headed?

I frowned. Maybe I should turn south a bit and look for some dragonkin for Spark. The hatchling was growing rapidly, and he couldn't follow me around forever. He needed to find his own kind and do dragon things, whatever that entailed.

Plus south would put me further from Anton. Not that I believed anyone would waste time coming after me. Unless the reward was very, very large, there should be nothing to worry about. Although...if the rumors were right, much seemed at stake this time.

I marked my original map to match Falk's, making a special note of two areas, Typhon and Echid, that he had etched with a skull and bones and something that might be a rat head. Both areas were north, tucked along a short mountain range. North was an area I wanted to avoid anyway. There was only one skull and bones area to the far south, so while west was the safest direction, I could still afford to drift south.

I oriented myself with the sun and headed onward.

By nightfall, the mountains loomed closer, but a solution to my problem didn't. How long could I be expected to stay huddled down in a forest in the middle of nowhere? I missed Grandmother and my sister Ava. And what if Uncle Ralph really had promised someone dragonsbane? Would Prince Irwin's father wait for the dowry containing such or would he move on to the next victim?

Grandmother swore that if I stayed away a year, it would give her time to make arrangements for us elsewhere.

"A year, Spark. That's a long time."

Spark sensed my distress and hopped alongside me. Then again, perhaps he just wanted me to scratch around the spikes growing out of his head. He had gone from duck-sized and scrawny to fatter, small dog-sized in the last day.

I ate dinner early, finishing the soft cheese. There was nowhere to go, and watching Spark polish off another squirrel was high on the list of avoidable entertainment. A more thorough search of the gift pack yielded a package of dried berries. "How did I miss these?" Luckily Spark didn't appear terribly interested in my treat.

One thing I had learned from the previous night: I was safer as a tree. After eating, I piled all my things near a few saplings and settled myself in. The ground was rockier here so it took longer to arrange my roots comfortably, but I stretched taller than the nearby bushes and trees with plans to steal the first rays of sunshine come morning.

I was already half dozing when Spark returned from his latest foray. It was good he was becoming more independent because no way could I hunt enough to keep him fed. He had barely landed when a very large hawk spiraled down, hopped along the ground in front of me, chirped a greeting and then launched himself back up and onto one of my branches.

I rustled my leaves at him, exasperated.

Spark had no such reservations. He puffed out a smoky greeting, complete with a happy wave of his spiked dragon tail.

I was tempted to show my face just to surprise Falk off his chosen branch, but such a display wasn't likely to catch him unaware given that he had managed to follow me all day or find me after I went dryad. *How did he know?*

Grumbling, I wobbled the branch he was perched on to express my lack of amusement.

He clucked a few chuckles and caressed my arm. His claws were like gentle tickles across my bark. The sensation resonated all the way into my very roots. When he ran one talon down the side of the main trunk, my face tingled in response.

"You'll not convince me with a pat on the head!" I yelled. Since my tantrum consisted of the noisy shaking of leaves, he was not properly cowed.

Hmph. If he didn't behave, I'd grow a stick right through his foot. Or one right above his head to swat him.

He subsided, but not without a chuckle that he quickly changed to a soothing, crooning melody.

Sometime before he stopped humming the low vibration I drifted into a peaceful slumber, relaxing into the forest around me. There were still no dreams, but the signals of the trees found me in sleep, whispering forest secrets, flashing pictures of a fox's den, the meandering of a raccoon and the warmth of soil wrapping me in safety.

The moon had only just risen when the forest noises changed. The gentle swaying of branches and the quiet animals shifted from a peaceful night to one with human voices and movement.

A stirring questioning of my leaves returned scents on the breeze and a leafy song from the other trees.

Men. Dragon.

Was it Lindis and Derrick? But he traveled as wolf. And the bristling of the forest indicated fear. The breeze passed along the smell of blood and sweat. The sounds evolved into grunting and panting, but stopped short of my copse.

"We coulda camped where we bagged it." A colorful description of his partner's mother and upbringing followed. "I swear on ale and whiskey, James, I'm not dragging this thing one step further in the damnable dark. We either git out the dragonsbane and make it walk or I catch forty winks and catch up to yer carcass in the morn."

"You know what happened the last time we camped where one of these things lived. If this one had a mate like that other one did, yer forty winks would be yer last."

The whining and panting was not put off by logic. "If we had waited until morn ta smoke it out, it wouldn't have mattered."

"Cripes, Vint, the one time we decided to wait until morning, the damn thing hunted us down and turned Mac into dragon fodder. Just get the fire going, would ya?"

By thinning my trunk and stretching a branch, I could just make out two forms not far from where I'd set my own fire a couple of hours ago.

Falk twittered uneasily, not liking what he was hearing.

Sure enough, the one called James found the remains of my fire. "Ssst. We got company."

The other voice wisely didn't answer, but joined him. They both touched the ashes. "Could be from last night."

"Maybe. Maybe not."

"Enough of this shit," Vint declared. "I'm gettin' the dragonsbane. The dragon can hunt down our supper and patrol. I ain't gonna do it."

"If all the damn ideas you spout were gold, we wouldn't need to blunder out here like fools hunting dragons for lazy-ass nobles. We gots eight dragons to herd across the border, and I ain't staying in this sewage of a kingdom to grow more of that weed. I damn near bin ate by rats and snakes, and ain't even seen ale since we got here."

These two close friends had to be the same ones who had attacked Spark's parents. There couldn't be men all over Wendal arguing about when to use dragonsbane and poaching dragons.

James started a cursory inspection of the woods, part of which involved checking their prisoner. He grabbed a sword and a mace before setting off.

The poor dragonkin lay on its side with a contraption that resembled a horse's halter looped through its muzzle and around its head. Scaled eyelids were at half-mast, and a parched, forked tongue was pushed out of its mouth by a glinting metal bar that kept its mouth locked half open. The sad creature had to be dead.

But the one called Vint had said something about making it hunt, and

James said they would be herding it across the border.

I grew the branch out until it was barely stable enough to remain straight, but the darkness defied me. Finally it occurred to me to ask the nearby trees.

It breathes. It bleeds from the metal in its mouth.

Once Vint got the fire going, I had better luck making out the details. The metal bar was not only shoved into the dragon's mouth, it pierced either side. If the dragonkin flamed its enemies, the bar would burn the unprotected tissues. In effect it would cook itself to death.

The beast was injured, tied to within an inch of his life, and the men had dragonsbane. It would be better off dead.

While James made ever wider circles, Vint nursed the fire using the remnants from my own camp. Once the flames were high, he untied a pack that was secured across the dragon's back. Muttering and still whining, he shoved aside a mace and grabbed what he wanted from the pack.

Cackling like an old, insane woman, he crooned to himself. "No sense in not using good help when you have it."

At the fire he rubbed his hands together over the flames, losing bits of dried pieces.

The fire jumped eagerly, snatching at the dust and puffing out black breaths of foul smoke. As the odor drifted towards us, there was a sharp stink of burning flesh and sulfur.

"Vint, I'm warning you!" James came tumbling back from his inspection. He let loose a stream of curses. "You are gonna burn yourself up with that stuff."

Indeed, Vint did seem mesmerized by the changing colors of the flames, giggling under his breath, sucking in mouthfuls of smoke. The captured dragonkin was no better. Its jaws were clamped nearly immobile, but it swayed and pulled against the rope at its throat, leaning into the smoke once the first wisps drifted near it.

Vint obliged the kin by untying the rope from the nearby tree. "Hunt. Disembowel. Bring food back. Go nowhere but after prey. Return. Return to the smoke."

The dragonkin dragged itself to the fire, one leg spasming and jerking roughly behind. It dipped its head into the flames, tasting the poison. The smoke thickened and billowed outward. Great puffs of it dispersed as the dragonkin stepped into the fire before turning to its task.

The smoke billowed outward, drifting between the trees.

With a sense of dread, I changed my leaves and bark, letting only low branches and leaves take in what fresh air could be found low to the ground.

Falk squawked weakly, a startled bird gasp. His feathers began shrinking as he changed, but his shift was not to conserve air, and it was not the usual smooth alteration. A wing that had been out for balance was suddenly a hand, but the arm was still winged. He grabbed at the branch above his head and missed. His body didn't respond properly, trapped as it was between bird and man.

Before he could recover, his head and torso shot up and talons that had held him in place were suddenly ungainly human feet, throwing his balance forward.

I flattened the branch beneath his feet, pulling in all of my mass except the branch holding Spark...only Spark wasn't there.

Spark!

The bulkier branch I grew under Falk gave him just enough time to wrap his fingers around it. He swung into me, hitting face first and hard before dropping to the ground.

I broke his fall, but not by much.

Spark chirped, a flat, but happy sound.

I sent the long branch back out, thin and fast like a growing vine.

No! My tree form groaned in despair. Spark sat in the middle of the fire, dancing and weaving in the smoke. He swayed to a song of flames that held him in a trance.

"Well, well, what have we here! James! We gots an extra!!"

Spark! RUN!

The trees could hear me, but the little dragon could not. If the other dragonkin was any indication, he'd obey my command, but I was not human, and it was too late to shout it. The men had already noticed him bathing in the flames.

Frantic, I shot a branch out in front of Falk to keep him from answering the call of the dragonsbane. It smacked him in the stomach, whip-like, but it was too flexible to stop him.

"Oof." He bent over from the force of my hit.

I shoved wood at the branch faster, making myself dizzy with the effort. What if he attacked me in order to reach the dragonsbane? What if the dragonsbane forced me to change and run into the fire?

Falk stumbled into my trunk, landing on his hands and knees. His lips kissed my bark, he was so close. "Shh, Drissa. Release me. I am not tempted to join them."

Was he lying? What was that stuff anyway?

He squeezed the thickening branch surrounding him, as if holding my hand.

"I'll not be leaving you," he whispered. "The change was my human brain taking over, recognizing the dangerous call to the hawk. It must have happened before when I dove into the ravine. I had to have nearly buried myself underground if it happened this fast."

Cautiously, I allowed the branch some slack.

Falk stayed right next to me, unmoving. I reeled it in further.

If anything, he crowded closer to me, tucking himself behind my bulk.

I changed the branch to low leaves, sprouting greenery where it would do the most good to keep him hidden. If the poachers set the larger dragonkin to hunting for anything other than a meal, we could be in serious trouble.

Spark was in very deep trouble already. Though it was still too early for nature's dew, drops of water dribbled down my bark, tears of worry. Spark was in the hands of the poachers, and he didn't even seem to know it. The dragonsbane had killed his instincts and held him in its thrall.

Chapter 9

The adult dragonkin did not take long to hunt. Even injured and missing several scales from being dragged, he returned with a large hare. It was disemboweled, but not skinned. Vint didn't seem to mind. He chuckled through cooking it, taunting Spark with the bones, not letting him eat. He tossed them to the dragon who had hunted instead.

"You'll learn," he cackled. "You do what you're asked and no more. Then you get fed."

That was quite enough for me. Silently, I began shifting back to human form. I would gut these two with my bare hands and snatch Spark right from the fire if necessary.

Falk, now that he was human, had recovered his balance. The short sword that had been strapped to his back was ready in his hand.

After collapsing silently next to him, it took me a few seconds to retrieve my own weapons from my pack.

Falk leaned in close. "We must wait."

I glared at him even though he couldn't see me in the dark. I shook my head fiercely, knowing he was close enough to feel the motion.

"There are more of them," he whispered.

We were too close to risk a conversation, but I leaned next to his ear anyway. "More? Where?"

"There are many more dragonkin missing or dead. That means there must be more men guarding the other missing dragonkin."

These two ill-born miscreants had talked of eight dragonkin. I fingered my dagger impatiently. Getting Spark back now didn't mean we couldn't find the camp with the other missing dragonkin later.

I hadn't asked enough questions at Derrick's house, but was smart enough to realize there was a complicated issue at hand. Tracking these two couldn't be as simple as it seemed on the face of things, or Falk and his friends would already have done so. None of them had been able to follow these two men after they killed or snatched Spark's parents.

What if this was our only chance to find the other eight dragonkin? What if Spark's mother or father was still alive in captivity?

Still, if I could get close enough to Spark and get a root around him...what then? Encase him in my trunk? Would he be able to breathe?

And would he make noise?

Oh, this was not going to be easy.

I stood, fully intending to inch closer and rescue Spark, and to hell with the consequences. Falk towered over me, either ready to help or perhaps to stop my foolishness, but the decision was taken from me.

The men had finished eating. "Ain't wasting the bane. We're almost out of it. Let's get'em moving."

The crooner protested. "We bin hunting this'n for a day and a half!"

"You're the one wasting the dragonsbane. No point in dragging them tomorrow morning after it's worn off. They're docile enough now. We'll be more'n halfway back before it wears off. Harness the little one and let's git goin'."

Neither man bothered to put the fire out, but it was dying anyway.

Vint repacked the few supplies he had taken out. "Don't move," he ordered Spark. He then tied the pack across Spark's back, but still didn't bother to feed him.

Spark was a growing dragonkin! He needed to hunt and eat. He hadn't ever had to carry anything. One stab with his sharp tail, and the guy would be a bloody mess, but Spark did nothing other than make a miserable gawping noise. He was in pain and confused.

James drilled out more orders, including instructions to flame any human or animal threats. His list of what he considered a threat was quite long. Then he pulled out a whistle and blew into it once. "You stay within hearing and when you hear it thrice, you land. Now fly due north."

Vint kept up a steady bit of his habitual whining, but now that he wasn't dragging or prodding the adult dragonkin, he seemed almost as willing to plod along as the drugged dragons. Each man carried a weapon and a pack of supplies smaller than mine.

Falk confirmed the reason they bothered to shoulder any weight. "The dragonkin cannot fly if too weighed down."

The two men plowed into the trees, using the stars to navigate.

We bided our time, me impatiently; Falk as still as the tree I could become.

Falk was quiet and quick in the woods, not to mention a better tracker than I, especially in the dark. The first time he attempted to take to the sky he couldn't shift properly, but an hour later he was able to scout from above, even though flying at night was a dangerous proposition.

After at least two hours of stumbling along, James called the dragons in to land.

When we heard the whistle, Falk and I backed off several paces in order to keep a safe distance.

If I hadn't been so worried I'd have been exhausted, but my nerves were on edge. I whispered to the trees, asking after Spark, but in my human form, the rustling of leaves was little more than murmurs confirming that they were ahead of us.

Falk crouched behind heavy brush and said in a low voice, "Several of us have tried to track the missing dragonkin, but had no luck. We knew the kin had often fought and were sometimes dragged away, but then they disappeared without a trace. We had no idea they were flying under compulsion."

"How did you know they were missing?"

Falk wrapped his hand around my forearm, perhaps to keep me from darting after Spark or maybe he meant to bolster my courage. "There's been far more than eight gone missing or turned up dead. The dragons noticed the disappearances first because several of the dragonkin have lairs in their territory. They tried tracking the missing kin, but at first assumed the kin had somehow escaped because the scent disappeared along the ground as though the kin had flown free. Then more went missing or turned up dead in their own lairs, and the dragons began to ask us what we might have seen."

My brain was stuck on "more than eight." What had the poachers done with the others?

Falk continued the history. "As soon as we began watching we noticed other lairs that had been disturbed or were mysteriously empty. The poachers probably tried to subdue the kin without a fight by using the dragonsbane, but it obviously didn't work every time. Kin are wary of strangers, and when the wind shifted against the poachers, they'd have a fight on their hands."

I thought about the ravine. "There must have been dragonsbane around where I found you. But it must not have been enough to keep Spark's parents from fighting because they were dragged from there."

"The smoke probably went straight up. I dove right into it."

The scent of burned sulfur and blood hadn't struck me as unusual even though I hadn't seen any signs of a fire. There was blood on the ground from a fight, and I had been standing next to a baby dragon. What else would it smell like? "There was no sign of a fire pit."

"No dragonkin would allow two men to wander into their territory and start a fire. If they carried a torch, they'd be limited to trying to force the smoke close enough to the dragon. When they attacked Spark's lair, I'm betting they only knew about one dragon. And if an unexpected dragonkin comes after you, you aren't going to stand around waiting for it to get a whiff of fumes. Those maces they carry could disable the dragonkin long enough to drag them off or force them to breathe the smoke."

It made barbaric sense. You try to drug the kin into compliance, but if you end up in a fight, you beat them senseless. You learn enough to know that another dragonkin can appear at any time, so you drag the kin away from the danger zone until you can use the dragonsbane to force it to help with its own kidnapping.

"Until you mentioned dragonsbane, we had no idea magic was involved. None of us suspected the poachers had a way to make them fly." He shook his head. "Once airborne, they were impossible to track."

"But the poachers? They don't fly!"

"No, but we are late to this game. Ofttimes the scents were old. Lindis told us there were humans involved, and we've been tracking closer and closer, which is how she and Derrick came across me so quickly after you rescued me. I wasn't the only one keeping an eye out, but we arrived too late."

"It might have been worse had you all had arrived earlier. What if they had used dragonsbane on all of you?"

His shoulders lifted in a shrug. "In any case, when Spark's lair was attacked, Lindis tracked the poachers with you leading the way. They only stopped when they found me."

"The poachers' days are surely numbered," I muttered.

"Not if they succeed in taking eight across the border. That is far outside our normal territories. We have almost no influence in the four kingdoms." He spread his hands. "Who knows when they will return? Who knows how many men are working with them?"

Even in a whisper, frustration and anger was evident in his voice.

I had nothing comforting to offer.

James and Vint rested and then tested the dragons' responses to commands. Finding it satisfactory, they sent them flying again.

We marched on, periodically stopping when the kidnappers called the dragonkin from the sky. I tried partially changing to tree in order to glean information from the forest ahead, but my communication skills were weak unless I went full dryad. It took my full concentration to ask questions, and the least distraction during an answer meant I had to start over.

Two hours shy of sunrise the kidnappers halted, calling the dragons down again. This time when Vint gave a command, the adult dragon didn't respond the way he wanted. Instead of continuing on, he yanked the poor thing to a nearby tree and tied it.

Spark was spared the piercing only because the halter they tried to force on him was too big. "Put the thing in his mouth anyway. If it fails to keep him docile, we'll use more dragonsbane."

Vint just giggled. "It's easier to get them back that way anyway."

I wasn't waiting for them to find a way to disfigure Spark or any other kin on my watch. Not if there was a chance of stopping them. I began plotting just how close I might be able to get before growing into a tree and rescuing Spark.

Falk took to the sky, while I shifted to oak. Thirstily, I drank, tasting more limestone in the water and perhaps the faintest taint of a settlement. Falk would know if we were close to such.

Meanwhile, I whispered to the trees, seeking answers—and for the first time, wondering if I were dryad enough to convince the trees to help me.

Chapter 10

After drinking my fill, I greeted my fellow trees. They were not quite as content or trusting as the ones a day's walk south of here. There were trickles of worry about fire and gnawing, minor complaints about fungus.

After we exchanged our grumbles about dangerous humans, the trees relaxed enough to inform me that owls flew, the dragonkin rested and the humans slept. That was the news I wanted to hear. Spark had flown all night. He had never gone that long without food, not since his hatching.

I thanked my new friends and promised to warn them of any imminent danger, hoping it was enough to begin the magic of cooperation.

I changed back and reached for my pack, but couldn't quite manage to extract the thing from between my ankles. Oh. In my exhaustion, I had failed to change my roots back to feet! Well, at least I was getting better at partial changes.

I forced food down, making sure to leave some out of the pack for Falk. He had been gone longer than expected. The sky was light in the east, a frustrating dawn. Had the men stopped earlier, darkness would have provided a better chance for sneaking near. Worriedly, I scanned the sky again, but there was still no sign of Falk.

Focusing on the problems I could potentially fix, I tried to change while keeping my dagger in my hand. Would I be able to use it to free the kin? Would they be quiet or put up a fight?

Spark knew me in both forms. He was a smart dragon. The kin understood human speech even if we couldn't return the favor. Sadly, neither kin had any trouble following orders once dragonsbane had been forced on them.

Another scan of the sky promised a warm day. The misty haze would burn off early. If something happened to Falk, I was on my own. The thought frightened me, which was silly. I'd only had his help for a day and a half, maybe two days if you counted the full night he spent in my tree.

How long would the men slumber?

There was no point in waiting longer.

Before I had done more than take a step, Falk returned, silently gliding to the ground before changing.

He didn't bother to stand; he remained crouched low. When he ran a tired hand through his hair, I noticed blood.

"What happened?" We were far enough away to risk low voices.

"I made contact with one of the owls. He'll get a message to Derrick and the others."

At my surprised look he said, "We birds talk to each other. I also caught four rabbits and dropped them to the kin."

"Oh, thank you!" I could have hugged him. Knowing that Spark had to be starved and suffering pained me greatly.

He smiled. I sank down beside him in the dirt.

"The men were dozing so I judged that feeding the kin was worth the risk. We need them strong enough to escape."

"This morning," I declared firmly.

To my surprise, he nodded. "I don't like where we are headed."

I didn't like it either, but probably not for the same reasons. "Why?"

"Did you study the map I provided?"

When I nodded, he said, "We don't have kingdoms here like you do across the border, but there are those who think we should be run that way. The place I marked with bones is a fiefdom run by the chimera and an old family of harpies. I'm hoping the poachers are headed to one of the surrounding slums rather than the larger fiefdom, Typhon, although it probably doesn't matter. Anything this close to the chimera territories means they are probably involved in some way."

"These chimera and harpies are shifters?"

"No, the chimera have the body and head of a rat, with an extra head that is ogre. They're constantly negotiating with the rest of us to make sure we don't consider them prey. Mostly, they excel at politics."

I groaned. "That can't be good."

"It's not. The harpies are partial shifters, but can't shift completely human. Now and then, there are some who try to fool us by shifting their wings completely and wearing hoop dresses, but the feet are always a dead giveaway. The chimera and harpies generally spend so much time arguing amongst themselves that they aren't much trouble for the rest of us. Lately though, they have lobbied to become a part of Wendal's council. Their goal has always been to take over the whole of Wendal, but so far, whenever they get out of hand, the dragons flame them into submission."

"We can't let them take Spark there!"

He agreed. "Rescuing him from one of their cities would be difficult. The harpies almost never leave the walls. It's rumored that most are too fat to fly, but regardless of the reason, they hold a position of power over the chimera. The chimera answer to their beck and call, and they can be a deadly adversary."

There was no time to waste. "I'll sneak close on foot and then turn tree. The dragonkin aren't under the influence of dragonsbane now, and if I can get the halters off—"

"How do you propose to do that?"

I shrugged. There were holes in my plan. "I have to try. The longer we wait, the worse it will be."

His scowl deepened. "If we can wait a couple of hours for the others to get here, taking the two poachers out will not be a problem."

"Only two hours?"

He glared at me. "It could be longer."

"We don't know how long the kidnappers will sleep. I'm getting Spark free of them." My fists clenched. Without meaning to, my chin raised in challenge.

"I'll be right behind you. If anything goes wrong, change to human and get yourself out of here."

I ignored that directive. "If I can get either kin freed, and no one is able to light any dragonsbane, it will work." In broad daylight, sneaking up on thieves and miscreants...we'd better hope the two poachers were deep sleepers.

We spent a few more minutes reviewing ins and outs of a plan. Just before we set out, Falk touched my arm. "One more thing. Watch for snakes. There's some very large dens around here. They like to go after rats that stray too far from the protection of the fiefdom."

"Snake shifters?"

He shook his head. "No, but they're big. Big enough to eat either of us if they happened to be hungry."

Well. Wendal had done what I never thought possible. Prince Irwin actually seemed the lesser of two evils. I shuddered. "Okay. Let's go."

Chapter 11

Falk went hawk, checked ahead and flew back to give me the okay. We crept forward slowly. Our timing was as good as it was going to get.

The dragonkin were separated by a few trees. Spark was trussed so tightly he could barely move. I had proposed cutting him free first; he knew me and wouldn't raise a stink. He also didn't have a metal rod shoved through his skin. I was deeply afraid that in freeing the other dragonkin, the poor beast might cry out, and that could be the death of us all.

I dropped low behind a hawthorn bush and then crawled, a dagger in my boot and one in my hand. My head was a gnarl of branches and leaves, the best partial change I could manage. Falk waited in a nearby tree, ready to create a distraction.

Halfway to my goal, James sat up. He stared at the dragons for just long enough that I grew a trunk and leaves. His eyes passed over me twice, stopping, studying.

What did he see? A fallen log with leaves? A strange face peering out from a short tree?

His head swiveled up, and he gazed into the branches above him.

What was he searching for? While he was distracted, I did everything but root. I added more leaves, blurred my face, and added roots to better grip the dagger.

Finally, grumbling, he lay back down, but he faced the dragons, watching them. I was nearly all tree, rooted enough to hold still. Even after his eyes closed, I dared not move.

Falk, bless him, took to the skies, flapping loudly enough that James turned and caught sight of him flying away.

James had his blade at the ready, but seeing the hawk set his mind back at ease. Perhaps he thought the bird landing had woken him.

I waited. Ten minutes. Fifteen. Spark's muzzled halter was tied closely to the tree and then staked into the ground. He could barely shift more than his talons. I had pictured Falk dropping a rabbit at Spark's feet for breakfast, but in order for Spark to have eaten, Falk had probably swooped past Spark's nose and dropped the food directly into his mouth.

Even the adult kin would have been forced to swallow the food whole because of the halter being secured so tightly. Belching fire and smoke would be nothing but sheer agony for the adult kin. From the scabs and dark drops beneath his head, it was obvious that the metal piercing the flesh on either side of his muzzle bled frequently.

I sent another silent thank you to Falk. If he hadn't already earned my trust, his willingness to right this wrong ensured it.

James twitched and half swallowed a snore. He hadn't snored earlier. He might be dozing. He might be faking it.

I changed one large root back to a foot and placed it carefully on the ground, one step forward. Problem. That was as far as I could go forward. The trunk piece attached to the foot was marginally capable of swaying, but there was no knee. Even if I formed a knee, it wasn't going to work like a knee.

Okay, fine.

I checked James. Uh-oh.

His eyes were open again. Something was bothering him. His searching glance passed over me. Stopped. Moved on again.

He was low to the ground though, and that gave me an idea.

I slowly pulled in my bulk, keeping branches that had been fingers around the knife. I pushed a root flat along the ground, snaking it forward. It was impossible to keep from making noise because there were twigs, leaves and dirt, but who would worry much about small animals rustling the leaves?

James, apparently. He reached for a short sword and settled it across his stomach.

If I tried to sleep like that, I'd roll over and spear myself.

Thankfully, speaking dryad was a silent thought rather than a noisy whisper. "*Talk*," I suggested silently. "*Make your leaves dance in the sunshine.*"

I was only a quarter dryad. Even when practicing, I had only had casual conversations with other trees, not asked favors.

A couple of the younger ash giggled, rustling branches, giving me the opportunity to push the root forward, closing in on Spark.

With James closing and then opening his eyes, it took forever for me to shrink from a half formed tree down to a stump with one long root.

Spark whined a small puff of smoke, shifting his head. His eyes rolled back, trying to keep me in sight.

I won't leave you, little one. Not this time.

When James opened his eyes and stared right at Spark, I used my free hand to extract the second knife from within my boot. That hand became another set of branches and a root headed for the adult dragonkin. We had one chance at this, and while James watched Spark, I'd move to the other kin.

But no matter what, I wasn't leaving Spark here.

When my branches holding the knife reached the adult dragonkin, I balanced myself by sending down another short root. Once stabilized, I snaked up to the halter, knife in branch. There was so little flexibility to these twigs that were not hands!

I switched my attention to Spark, rooted myself for balance, and then prepared. To do this, I was going to have to change the branches to hands over the long distance. It wasn't possible to sweat in tree form, but there was definitely pressure that needed out. My head felt as though it might split from the efforts of changing and growing various parts.

Twigs back to hands...the bark...shifted to skin, but the wood remained solid. I gasped for air through my leaves, nearly passing out. I couldn't do this. It was impossible.

I breathed deep, waiting for the forest around me to stop fluttering in and out of focus. Whispering trees voiced concern around me, but there was no time for reassurances.

I switched my attention to the larger dragon, sliding the branches that were not fingers up to the halter. I forced the knife underneath, but froze in horror when the knife caught on exposed dragon skin left raw by missing scales on his muzzle.

The dragonkin never flinched. One eye watched me and the other watched Spark, reminding me that Lindis had spoken mind-to-mind with Spark.

I hoped Spark told this guy I was friend because from this distance, I couldn't discern a way to free the pin holding the metal bar. Luckily the rest of the halter was like any horse halter with straps of leather holding it around his muzzle.

The knife was between the leather and the dragon, but my branches were thin and weak. How to flex and pull?

I wrapped my branches and tugged, twisting the knife and praying I didn't cut the dragon's muzzle off. When a drop of blood hit one of my branches, I was ready to cry.

The dragon had no such reservations. Bleed or not, he yanked and sawed his face against the blade, snapping the first piece of leather.

The knife bounced against the nearby walnut tree and knocked a chunk of bark to the ground. Whoops. I was not making any friends today.

The tree grumbled a deep protest.

Sorry, friend.

The metal bar still pierced the dragon's jaw, but he had more movement than before. I managed to retrieve the knife and slice one of the leathers that bound the halter to the tree before turning back to Spark.

The little dragon wasn't as tightly secured by the halter because it was too big for him, but there was an extra strap around his muzzle that had to be cut.

I sawed away.

James stood up with a grunt, his sword at the ready. He eyed the dragons, but instead of heading for one of them, he went between them, right for me.

Scared to stillness, I hardened my bark, waiting for the blow as he raised his sword and swung it down fast.

Using the sword like a broom, he swept at the leaves. "Damn snakes." He made another pass, stepping on the part of me that led to Spark. As soon as he felt the shape of the root under his foot, he jumped back and hacked harshly at the ground, just missing me.

He cursed as he realized he had just attacked a tree root. "Sstt. Vint. These woods are full of snakes. Slithering. Slithering in the leaves."

Another critical mistake on my part. My convincing a few trees to rustle and giggle had backfired, keeping him awake rather than soothing him to sleep. I was going to get us all killed.

James wiped the back of his hand across his mouth. "Vint! Git yer carcass in gear. I ain't staying here." He kept a wary eye on the ground while he sheathed his sword and then extracted an incense burner from a leather bag secured around his waist.

Vint gurgled a half-asleep response, his face behind his pack. I frowned. That pack hadn't been there before. When had he moved it from his feet to his head? And was he closer to the tree behind him than he had been before?

James either didn't notice or didn't care about Vint's lack of response. He carefully extracted a handful of crushed herbs and dusted them into the incense burner. "Vint, I'll leave your arse here to sleep it off and get et by snakes!"

Without waiting on Vint, James stalked over to the banked fire and dropped the metal canister into the burning coals at his feet.

Time had run out.

Chapter 12

The tails of both dragonkin were staked on either side to the ground. With his head freed from the tree, but still muzzled, Spark might be able to chew through the leather around his spiked tail, but he remained still as a statue.

Was he waiting for a signal or was he somehow bound by another part of the halter?

I snaked the first root to the tail of the full grown kin and slashed, a tree limb in the throes of a windstorm.

Less concerned about discovery now, I tried to change fully human, cut through the leather straps with my twig arm, and shuffle closer all at the same time.

Both dragons feared the smoke. James didn't waste time crooning or giggling. As soon as the incense caught, he snatched it from the fire.

He headed our way, swinging it back and forth purposefully.

I had feet and hands and one arm. The rest was tree. The hand trying to free Spark's tail was too much tree, and couldn't saw back and forth. I tried to force fingers, but I was spread too thin.

James was heading straight for Spark, rather than the older dragon.

In desperation, I stabbed at the leather, but lost my grip on the dagger. "Oohnooo!" I had mouth enough to groan, but it came out sounding like a howl of wind through the trees.

James stopped in his tracks, staring right at me. Picking up the dagger was impossible. My twig fingers batted at it uselessly. From not too far away, a hawk screamed a war cry and warning all at once.

My body pulled insistently as I desperately tried to change parts. Pain jerked across my limbs, right down to bone. I couldn't go human this spread out. It was the wrong shape. What made sense for a dryad did not for a human.

I fled back to myself, pushing and shoving like a flood trying to squeeze into a pipe all at once.

Spark's eyes rolled in his head, and he squealed in fear as the smoke drifted his way.

As I rolled back to myself, I saw the adult dragonkin flick his tail, struggling to tear the leather I had nicked with the knife. One part of the halter kept his head from full movement.

James had stopped advancing. He stared at me as I changed.

As I reached full human, panting and dizzy from my efforts, he recognized me as human.

"Hey!" He stared stupidly. "You're a tree!" He raised his sword, but continued to stare without moving. "You're...the one betrothed to Prince Irwin along with the dragonsbane we promised!"

Well, chicken crap. He not only knew what I was, he knew who I was. "Don't blame me for your crimes," I snarled. My hand still gripped one dagger, and I stood, determined. If I could get to him before he turned the dragons on me...

"Vint! We gots the mother lode here! How big was the bounty for the girl?" As the idea took shape in his pea-brain, he waved the incense burner, reminding himself of his original task. "But yer uncle might not pay for your return this late. He's already promised your little sister instead." James barked a laugh that held no amusement. "Who wants to be betrothed to a damn hunk of wood?"

He took the final step towards Spark, but the smoke was rising as smoke was wont to do. Spark was just over a foot tall, unlike his fellow captive whose head would top mine easily.

James leaned in.   The wind wafted the smoke closer to Spark's muzzle.

"Spark! Fight! Flee! Do not listen to a command from James or Vint!"

James' eyes flicked to me as he realized I had at least a basic understanding of the dragonsbane.

Either because Spark had breathed the incense or because he was smart enough to fight anyway, the little dragon obeyed me, shifting his muzzle away. As soon as he moved his head, he realized part of the halter was cut. He reared back. One side of the halter was still secured around the tree, but the bar fell from his mouth as he wiggled. He then belched a flame so miserably small, it wouldn't have lit a candle.

James laughed. He reached with his arm away from his body, still waving the incense. "You'll listen to me!"

"Do not obey anything from James or Vint," I shouted again.

Instead of rushing to Spark, I scrambled to the other dragon. As I slashed at leather pieces, I saw Falk hoist Vint over a tree limb. The miscreant dangled from his ankles like a butchered deer.

"Free your tail! Avoid the smoke!" I screamed at Spark.

But he had gotten a whiff of the dragonsbane. His head swayed back forward in search of more. Still, my words were a command he was compelled to obey.

James let loose a roar that would have done either dragon proud. He had expected me to run to Spark, but I was no idiot. James was twice my size, he had a sword to my dagger, and he carried lethal smoke that could force Spark to turn against me.

With fingers and arms functioning at last, I slashed the remaining piece of halter from the adult dragonkin. Rather than study the metal mouthpiece, I dove for his tail, sliding the dagger under the leather tie and yanking upwards.

I rolled away in the nick of time. This dragonkin had not breathed any smoke. This dragon was older, wiser and fully aware of his weapons. He may not be the size of a war horse, but he was easily the size and strength of a full-grown wolf.

James didn't have time to drop the incense burner and fully raise his sword.

Chapter 13

The dragonkin did not eat James, but he tore him into enough pieces there wasn't anything left but ant fodder.

I trusted Falk to watch my back while I finished freeing Spark. The idiots had wrapped the harness so tightly, it was no wonder Spark hadn't realized he was partially freed. His face had gone numb to anything other than pain. One loop around his neck was so taut, the knot had to be cut rather than undone. Pulling on it any further might very well have suffocated him.

When the restraints were finally removed, it was a bedraggled dragonkin that pushed his face into my knee. "Can you hunt?" I asked softly. "I know you are hungry."

His scales were as dull as a tarnished tankard with no sign of their usual iridescent silver and blue.

A half roar of protest from the larger dragonkin drew my attention.

Falk stood well to the side of the prisoner, but faced the kin. With his neck stretched, the enraged beast was only just taller than Falk, but much more deadly. Saliva and smoke burbled from his mouth. His scales were as dull as Spark's, and one eye spun wildly as if the agony of his wounds had to somehow escape.

"I won't tell you not to kill him." Falk kept his voice soft. "But there are others of your kind in captivity. It may be prudent to leave this one alive for now so that he can lead us to the others."

Vint gargled a noise between a gag and a spit. The thin noose around his neck kept his complaints to a minimum.

The dragonkin roared another protest, the fire in his belly eager to ignite. Only the metal bar kept him from screaming his rage and toasting everything in sight.

If the poor beast were to attack Falk in some crazed attempt at revenge...I clenched my dagger, but it was useless. Falk would die. I could not even stop a small dragon like Spark, let alone a larger one.

"Spark, is the smoke still controlling you?"

The little dragon whimpered in confusion. I feared letting him hunt in his weakened condition. If I told him to hunt, he would obey me, but he might kill himself trying. If I could get both of these dragons food...

I sighed. "Oh, for pity's sake. You are hungry, you want to hunt and you have no idea if you can hunt. And your friend is too angry to hunt." The adult dragonkin swiveled its head my way.

One wrong move might encourage the adult dragonkin to attack, so we stood there, all of us huffing and puffing and miserable.

Thankfully, the standoff was solved in the form of Lindis landing. She assessed the scene in an instant. Her voice was gravel and brimstone. "Takkar would like you to remove the mouth torture. I'll bring food."

She paused only long enough to deposit Zoe before launching back to the skies. I spun around looking for the wolf because where Zoe went, the wolf would also be.

Derrick drifted in front of a thicket just long enough to be seen before continuing reconnaissance or killing off evil trolls or whatever it was that wolves did in this situation.

Zoe was already by Takkar's side by the time I gathered my wits enough to drag myself over. My leg hurt as if I had stretched it too far in tree form. My wrist was sprained from flopping about with the dagger. I was lucky the other arm wasn't broken from where James had stepped on it. The bruise was going to be nasty and deep.

While Zoe worked on the metal bar, I used my good hand to slash the last of the leather restraints off. "I'm sorry I couldn't figure out how to get the pin out," I apologized to the dragon. "There wasn't enough time." I unbuckled the harness around his neck and middle that had been there for the packs.

"This pin is stuck," Zoe complained. "I think it was pounded in there, as if they never intended to take it out!"

Takkar grunted and wiggled to no avail. Falk finally came over to lend his muscle.

Zoe frantically grabbed items from her pack. It was still secured tightly about her waist as if she traveled by dragon often enough to automatically secure important items to keep them from flying off.

"I can blast the thing off with a small spell," she muttered. "But I don't want to hurt the dragonkin. Oh, here." She handed me a bottle. "Lindis brought this in case the dragonkin were wounded."

Takkar had slash wounds and missing scales. Spark was half starved. Physically, he hadn't suffered more than a few abrasions. While Zoe and Falk worked at the pin, I rubbed the salve on the injuries.

Lindis dropped an entire deer on what had been the campfire as she glided back down.

The wolf came out of the woods to help with the pin, and I finally sat down in complete exhaustion. I hadn't slept in far too long. I'd barely eaten. If I hadn't gone tree a few times where water was available, I'd probably be dehydrated. I flexed my wrist, wondering if it was broken or merely sprained.

Propped against a motherly oak, I watched Spark eat. Instead of gobbling his food, he tore off chunks. He ate in a half daze as though seeing the food through a fog. The dragonsbane hadn't worn off.

When Takkar was free of the pin he ate too, but his mouth bled, and every bite had to hurt as much as the need to eat.

With the camp almost under control, Falk joined me. His hair remained tied back out of the way, but we could both use a bath.

I handed him some cheese and the waterskin. "We have to free the others," I said.

Vint still swayed upside down from the tree limb.

Falk nodded, holding the cheese, but too tired to eat it. "Lindis has a plan. We have to find the kin before we can free them."

"When did you...secure Vint?"

He smiled. "Right after I flew off. I came back, got in close by hopping nearby and then changed. I dropped a garrote around his neck. He never saw me coming, although the noise I made may have been what set James off."

I disagreed. "It was the forest. I told the trees to whisper and talk. James thought the noise was snakes. Plus, I was growing along the ground, slithering right along in a manner that could easily have been a snake. I'm lucky he didn't hack off one of my roots."

"Will you help us?" he asked without looking at me.

I blinked. "Well of course. I not going to abandon the rest of the dragonkin!" I was angry that he would think so low of me.

"What about your sister? James said she has been promised in your stead." His head swiveled to face me, his eyes red from weariness, but no less intense.

I felt a ridiculous urge to wipe at least some of the sweat and dirt from my face, but any attempt would only smear it more. My roots and branches had been rolling in leaves and crawling through soil. I was dirty from head to toe, worried sick and yet, there was a chore here that had to be finished. "Grandmother will watch her back." With the words, my fear ratcheted up. Grandmother was formidable, but not even she could stop politics. Being sold to a prince might not be a much better future than being a captured dragonkin.

Falk wrapped his hand around my clenched fist. "When we have freed the dragonkin, I will help you find your sister. You have my promise."

I fretted for the next hour that Falk had told everyone about my dryad ability. Not that escaping Lindis or the others seemed necessary, but the secret had allowed me to rescue Spark. It bothered me that James had guessed because that meant that Uncle Ralph had spread the word. Fiend. He'd sell any family secret to the highest bidder. Hell, he'd sell to *any* bidder.

Zoe came over, muttering. She held out some fresh bread, along with my old set of clothes. "You hang around us too long, and you'll find you have to start leaving stashes of clothing all over the forest like everyone else."

"Really?" I accepted both things gratefully, putting the clean leathers in my pack for later. "I didn't know anyone here wore real clothes. Everyone seems to dress in partial skins of their other self."

She smiled. "When they do take the time, you should see the stitching. My mother is a seamstress and after visiting for the wedding, she designed a whole new trend of pants that have removable leather seams. It's really catching on in Birk, too."

"Removable?"

"The pants are laced together at seams rather than sewn, so that when the shifters change suddenly, it snaps the leather lacing, rather than tearing the clothes. You can just lace the pieces of clothing back together rather than having to sew a whole new outfit. Mom invented halters for weapons that stretch, too. We used regular leather straps and special cloth that I strengthened with a spell."

"And the weapons halter stretches to fit the shape of the shifter?" I thought of the short sword Falk carried across his back whether flying or walking.

"Exactly. If Derrick needs to carry a weapon while wolf, he can wear the harness and it will shrink or expand as he changes shape."

"And that works?"

"Most of the time, although we're still tweaking both inventions. Lindis tends to have these rather explosive shifts, and more often than not, she rips the holes where the lacing needs to go. She doesn't need to carry extra weapons, but she does love her sword, so the stretchable harness has proven to be one of her favorite pieces."

"She is rather large as a dragon." My eyes went to Spark. He had finished eating for the moment. When he saw me watching him, he squeaked weakly, looking lost. "You can come over here, Spark. You can do what you want. No waiting for orders."

Happily, he waddled over. He had managed to eat enough to about double his size again, but this time it was all in his belly. I hoped he didn't start anything on fire by accident while he digested the food.

As he settled near my leg, Zoe inspected his scraped scales. "He'll be okay. The dragonsbane will wear off. I've been studying it. Those bastards."

"What is it?"

"It's a wolfsbane plant, which is normally only poisonous to the wolves. But after reading the grimoire, I think the idiots are growing it using dragon's blood in place of water or fertilizer or both. You'd think that would only make it poisonous to dragons, but dragon magic is powerful stuff. Once dragon blood feeds the plant, it adds various magical properties, most of which the gryphon's notes didn't bother to cover because he didn't have enough opportunity to study the entire range."

"Can dragonsbane kill Spark? And the wolves?"

Zoe shivered. She was as horrified about the dragonsbane as me. "I'm not sure, but wolfsbane by itself is not good for wolves. I'd not have figured any of this out except that last year a gryphon ensnared Lindis. I knew he had something of hers—blood or hair or something. I'm betting now it was blood that he used to grow dragonsbane to use directly against her."

"She escaped though."

"Barely. The dragonsbane was stored in a ring. He spelled the ring with a command so that if she wasn't wearing the ring, she couldn't turn dragon. The ring was also a call to her dragon, which meant it forced Lindis to answer the call."

I thought about Falk falling out of hawk. "Dragonsbane messes with their ability to shift. How do we stop it?"

Zoe sighed. "I'm not sure. This time around it looks as though someone is using dragonkin blood, not dragon's blood. It's not as potent, but it was probably a lot easier to kidnap or kill a dragonkin than a real dragon."

Watching Lindis secure the camp and threaten the prisoner twice to get answers, it was obvious that anyone with a brain would stay well away from dragons. What fool had tried to control a full-grown dragon? I didn't have to ask what might have happened to him. Whoever he was, I bet he was burned to a crisp. "Way less risky."

Zoe nodded emphatically. "When Lindis didn't have the ring, whoever held it could partially control her. Not entirely; she's still very human and that part of her brain was capable of fighting the spell, but it was terrible to behold. The dragonsbane they are using now is most potent against the kin, but it still seems to affect the shifting ability of the others."

I squeezed the top of Spark's head. His horns hadn't grown any in the last day or so. I scritched around them carefully. "We have to stop them from planting anymore dragonsbane."

Zoe nodded. "Do you need anything else to eat?"

Before I could answer, Spark lifted his head from his half-doze. He gave a hopeful puff.

We both laughed. "Spark, I don't think you have room." I gave him a piece of bread anyway.

As we stood to join the others, Lindis stomped over. "I'm going to take word back to council. We'll use that scum-piece to track and find the others. He confessed."

That was one way of describing him screaming answers to her questions when she flamed his feet, and threatened to cook his eyeballs and then eat them. I doubted she actually intended to eat anything belonging to such a disgusting creature, but controlling a pinpoint flame to do her exact bidding? Not a doubt in my mind.

"Falk has insisted you go with him to his roost. I'll take you there, if you are willing. You could walk, of course, but that will only delay things."

"When...what about the other dragonkin?"

"After I bring the council up to date, we'll return with reinforcements. Not a single dragonkin will remain in slavery."

"Spark's parents might be there." I stroked his little head carefully. "We need to rescue them if we can."

She snarled, but I didn't take it personally. "You're not in shape to do it now."

She was right, of course. Exhaustion was a dark tunnel calling me. I could barely see what was right in front of me and the pain in my arms made me not even care. Spark had eaten, but he needed rest and more food, not necessarily in that order.

"Falk will walk with you or I can fly you. There's no point in wasting time walking," Lindis said again.

"I have my things. Spark, can you fly with us?"

He gave a sleepy chirp.

"Be right back." Lindis and Zoe went to confer with Falk and Derrick. Derrick and Zoe would stand guard here, while the rest of us prepared.

Zoe started walking a circle, mumbling a spell under her breath.

I joined Falk. "Where do you live?" I envisioned being dropped into a giant nest on the side of a cliff, completely at Falk's mercy, unable to leave unless I chose to rappel down the side. What if I fell? And what was this nest made of anyway? I wasn't going to get much rest sleeping on a bunch of sticks. I sighed. Then again, maybe I could just turn tree and bed down with the rest of the branches.

"Thank you for coming home with me," he whispered in my ear.

I was startled out of my train of thought. "What?"

"I don't wish to leave you here although you would be safe enough with the wolf." He scowled at the idea.

"They are your friends, right?"

He nodded. "Of course."

My eyes narrowed. "Did you tell them about me?"

He watched me thoughtfully for a moment, and then a small smile crept across his face. "No."

"How did you know about my dryad, anyway?"

His smile got bigger. "Your beauty was such that it did not escape my notice even in your other form?"

I scowled. "I'll figure it out. I'm still learning, you know. But Grandmother is a pedantic teacher. I cannot believe she left out a single trick."

He chuckled quietly, reminding me the tiniest bit of a magnificent bird caressing my arms. "I am very glad you have decided to stay with me."

I wondered if this nest of his had running water. "Where do you live, now that I've already committed to flying there on the back of a temperamental dragon?"

He tilted his head at the suspicion in my voice. "I doubt you have been through the area, or I would have already noticed you. My main tree is in the Redwood Forest. Don't worry. Lindis knows its location, and it's on the way back for her. She has business with the council. She's meeting with the ogres."

"The chimera?"

"No, the full ogres. They are none too pleased with their distant relatives allowing and possibly abetting the kidnapping of the dragonkin. Nothing happens this close to chimera territory without them knowing about it. The ogres wish to be in on the raid to rescue the kin. Lindis will drop you off at my tree before taking care of the other business."

"Oh." Well, at least his home wasn't on the side of a cliff. Probably not if it was in a tree.

Chapter 14

Spark tried to fly with us, but after the first few flaps, Lindis plucked him from the air with one giant claw and flipped him over onto her back.

Gratefully, he settled behind me. He may have eaten too much of the deer. Between the ordeal he'd just been through and being weighed down by all that food, he'd probably fly straight into a tree if left to his own wings.

I wasn't sure what it said about me that he perched behind me and used me as a windbreak. "You're too big to sleep on my pack, Spark."

He was. But he rested his head there and chirped out meaningless happy sounds as Lindis soared through the air faster than he'd probably ever flown. My first trip with Lindis had been in the dark, thus speed had been nothing more than an impression of wind. This time, the landscape moved beneath us, a blur of shapes and colors. Mountains danced off to my right and for the first time I glimpsed what might be larger settlements.

She headed for redwoods, a stand of trees that in their own way competed with the mountains for majesty and size.

Falk had not lied. Lindis set me down in front of one of the redwoods. It was larger than a small castle. The magnificent limbs even formed turrets when you considered the giant branches that curved and reached for the sky.

"I'll be back," Lindis said. The flap of her wings as she departed almost knocked me over.

We had flown higher than Falk so I had no idea whether he had already arrived or not. Tentatively, I reached out with one hand and touched the redwood. Warmth spread through me along with a feeling of great age, contentment and strength.

Goodness. I'd never met a timber so old!

The redwood didn't appreciate that thought. *Venerable. I am* not *old.*

"Of course not," I corrected myself, speaking both aloud and in dryad. The dryad part was still a bit of a struggle when I wasn't changed. "No more than five hundred...*five hundred? Really?*"

The redwood grumbled again, a vibration I not only heard with my ears, I felt with my hands and my feet.

"You must be very wise." I did not have to fake the admiration in my voice.

"Thank you," Falk said with a mischievous grin as he opened the door. "Welcome."

"I wasn't talking to...oh, never mind." I was too tired to risk insulting my host. Either of them. I'd already come close enough with the giant heartwood.

On my way inside, I tripped over the root that served as part of the door frame. Falk just about missed catching me as I stumbled by, but even exhausted as he was, he snagged the back of my pack and kept me from landing on my face.

"Thanks." I righted myself and turned to make sure Spark was following, but he was not. Sometime after I started conversing with Redwood, he had curled up in a sunbeam and was now snoring lightly.

Falk smiled and closed the door gently.

The inside of Redwood was cozy, reminding me of my grandmother's cottage in the woods where she had lived before Father died. The room smelled of fresh forest with just a hint of spices. A black wood stove was tucked into a corner. Off to the side, a table that was part of the tree curved out of the hardwood floor. Heartwood wound up and around, flattened into shelves along one entire side of the room. Near the table, a wooden bench and two chairs grew out from the floor. "This. Is. Gorgeous."

"I imagine you can appreciate it more than most."

Redwood preened even more than Falk.

"I've never seen...this is utterly amazing."

Falk never took his eyes off of me. "Yes. It is." After a significant pause, he added, "I am glad you came. You needn't stand there holding your pack as if you're ready to run out the door. Be at home here."

I blinked, caught by the intensity of his eyes. I wasn't ready to run; I had just been too stunned by Redwood to do anything but stare. Be at home here? This was...this was too incredible to be home! I couldn't imagine being lucky enough to live in a place like this, and Falk was looking at me as if he meant his welcome for always, as if we were lifelong friends, or... "You're crazy," I told him.

"Probably." He smiled and stepped back. "There's a tub and shower behind that door. I'll find some food while you clean up, and then I'll take my turn." He cocked his head. "Normally I'd say look around if you need something, but I suspect you can actually ask the house?"

I grinned. "I'll be fine. This is better than..." I'd been about to say "home" but Uncle's castle hadn't ever really been home, and I'd been thinking of the old castle, the one that had been home. "This is a great place to be." I knew in my core that I was safe here, not only because of Redwood but because of Falk. He had asked me here rather than leave me standing in a forest alone. And he had promised to help me find Ava.

"Thank you." Before I fell apart or asleep, I scurried off in the direction of the shower.

Like Derrick's place, there was not only running water, there was hot water. If the dragonkin had already been rescued and my sister safe, I might have stayed in the shower for the rest of my life.

When I finally did step out of the water, it was to the sound of arguing. Frantic, I retrieved my dagger from my pack. Redwood was already reassuring me that the muted voices were not enemies. They weren't shouting, but they were angry.

I rested my hand against the smooth walls in order to hear better.

It's not polite to spy.

"It's not all that polite to argue about me, either," I muttered, having heard enough to realize that someone was not happy about me being here.

You dress. I'll spy.

I had no idea what that meant, but since I was the guest and had been reprimanded by a five-hundred-year old redwood, I removed my hand. As soon as I did so, the thick wood changed and the voices were as clear as though we were standing together in the same room. That had me dressing in my clean leathers in a hurry. Even if Falk and...his father? They weren't in the room with me, but their voices made it seem as if they were close enough to reach out and touch me.

"We've had nothing but problems from across the border. Bringing one here isn't very smart."

"I didn't bring any problems. Neither did she."

"Maybe if she had just married the prince, we wouldn't have to go rescue a bunch of dragonkin from the chimera and their new friends!"

"Like you want me to just marry your choice? That's what this is all about, isn't it? My answer was no before, and it's still no. I'm not marrying for your convenience, Father."

Well, now Redwood had to reform again because both men were yelling. I'd be lucky if I didn't step out into a room full of swords. Or claws and beaks if they decided to go at it in their version of fisticuffs.

"Briella is beautiful. She's talented and—"

"And our marriage would be a perfect boon for the two largest clans, making us as powerful on council as the dragons, yes, I know. The answer is still no, and Drissa coming here just meant her uncle found someone else to marry the prince. He still promised the dragonsbane, which is almost as dangerous to us as it is to the dragonkin. Maybe we should work on solving that problem rather than worrying about promises I will not make."

Okay, this was getting way too personal. I moved to open the door. It was stuck. "Very funny," I grumbled.

A cool breeze at my back had me swiveling quickly. What had been a smooth tree wall on the other side of the bathroom was now an open doorway. "Who would have guessed that living in a tree would have so many surprises? Must be a barrel of laughs for guests who get up in the middle of the night to visit the facilities."

Your grandmother would tell you to have more respect for your wise elders. Falk endures an old argument, and it is not yours to interrupt.

I grinned, because Redwood had the phrasing exactly right. Grandmother had always told me to know the difference between age and wisdom and not to assume that everyone older than me was also wiser. I peered through the new opening. Roots wound downward in a beautiful spiral staircase.

Slinging the pack across my tired shoulders, I took the stairs.

Chapter 15

Below ground Redwood had a much more elemental atmosphere. Roots tangled every which way even after I reached the cavernous bottom. A small pool glimmered under a canopy of underground boughs. Light filtered in from above; at least Redwood allowed it to do so right now. The pool bubbled from underground before turning into a small stream that disappeared under more giant roots. The wonderful scent of water and rich earth was a heady perfume.

I stared in wonder at the cavern, my hand still holding onto Redwood for balance. Falk was a lucky man. Grandmother would be in awe of the place, and she was a difficult lady to impress. The thought made me sad all at once. Grandmother might be bound in a dungeon for all I knew. There was much work ahead. I hoped we would be in time. We had to be.

Work can wait until after dormant time...sleep, Redwood corrected himself.

It didn't take me long to locate a lovely mossy ledge near the pond. I'd certainly slept on worse and harder beds. The pack made a fine pillow and wrapped in my cloak, I drifted to sleep listening to the tinkling of water and the rush of life gushing through Redwood.

* * *

Waking up underground imparted no sense of time of day, especially when the only light came from softly glowing moss. Either the sun wasn't up or Redwood had decided not to filter light through his roots today.

I yawned, stretched and took inventory of my aches and pains. My wrist was the most bothersome, and sleeping curled up and motionless had only added to the stiffness. I bathed it and my face in the pool before heading up the stairs.

The smell of bacon assaulted my senses before I was done in the bathroom. Feeling half shy and completely starved, I opened the door. This time it didn't stick in the least. I stuck my tongue out at Redwood as I passed through the arch.

"You know, I lived here two years before I discovered the pool and cellar. My own home didn't deem it necessary to share that information for two years, yet you were here less than two hours and were offered a bed and bath."

I beamed. It was nice to know Redwood liked me, at least a little. Falk, however, scowled as though this news were of the highest insult.

Spark bounded to my side and squeaked. It was probably meant to be a full greeting, but his mouth was full.

"I had to have Spark come inside to track you down." Falk waved a spoon at me from his position over the stove.

I really wanted some of what appeared to be hot milk, but Grandmother had always said that if you must fight a bear in the morning, do it first and with skill, or it could ruin your entire day. Ava and I always laughed when she said it about Father, but it was not a joke at all when she said it about Uncle Ralph.

I smiled. Falk was much more like Father than Uncle Ralph. When Grandmother and Father sparred neither won, but both seemed to gain an advantage from the exercise. "I think Redwood would have told you had you asked."

Falk raised an eyebrow. "I don't talk to trees like you do."

I shrugged. "It wouldn't have mattered. Redwood understands you. He would have shown you." I looked at the magnificent carvings surrounding us. "Probably."

"If that is true then why did it take two years before it...before he showed me the cellar?"

Well, now. That was an interesting question. Falk seemed truly out of sorts this morning. "Maybe you didn't need to know. Besides, time progresses differently for trees. And yours is very—venerable." I stopped myself from saying "old" just in time. "Plus, I'm a distant relative. Very distant," I added, because I was only a quarter dryad and didn't want to insult Redwood by implying he was too closely related to one of such low stature.

"And how did you get to the cavern without coming out of the bathroom?"

I grinned. "Redwood made a door for me."

Falk shook his head in disbelief. He stared at me for so long, I had to say, "I think you're burning breakfast."

Since he had forgotten to offer me any, I edged over to the milk warming on the back of the stove.

Falk flipped the sizzling bacon onto a plate and pointed with his chin to a shelf containing a row of assorted chipped mugs.

I helped myself.

He added some milk to his pungent licorice coffee. "For a long time I believed I carved this tree into home."

I sat and stared hungrily at the table full of breads, cheeses and fruits.

"Mother brought enough food this morning for twelve people to make up for Dad pitching another one of his fits." He waved his hand at it. "We'll be able to take plenty of supplies today."

Again, I helped myself. "Redwood says...and I heard, uhm. Your father doesn't seem very happy that I am here."

"Don't be fooled. Neither is Mother. Dad is the bully; Mother uses bribery."

Tasting the sweetbread without even spreading any butter on it, I could definitely say his mother's method was preferred. "Wow. I'd give into a lot of arguments to have these for breakfast every day."

"Don't you start! I'm not marrying Briella just to make *you* happy every morning of our lives!"

I stopped chewing. "That would be..." I giggled. "Awkward."

His face burned an interesting shade of dark red. "Maybe I'll run away to Anton. No one would bother me there as I doubt Prince Irwin would insist on marrying me."

I laughed outright. "You'd probably be safe from him. But as soon as the marriage mart found out about your talents and loyalty, you'd have all kinds of offers, some more forceful than others."

"Hmph."

I swallowed my laughter and sighed. "It was cowardly of me to run. But there were no good options." The idea of Falk being forced to marry someone annoyed me. Not that I was protective of him. We weren't even friends, not really. We were just bound by circumstances, especially if I didn't count the promise he had made to help rescue Ava. Apparently he was not quite so free to keep that promise. He had other obligations.

Falk's morning grumpiness was fast catching up to me.

"You running was not cowardly," he said.

"It was. Had I not run off, Ava wouldn't be in trouble now." I dropped my gaze, guilty.

Falk reached across the table and lifted my chin. "No one here is going to hog-tie anyone to a wedding. I am certainly not about to sit around and wait to be dragged into a marriage of convenience. Father has been selecting brides for me since I was six. It's only this last one where Mother got involved. She may bribe to her heart's content, but she can't force me to marry anyone."

"Are you sure?"

He frowned. "Of course I'm sure!"

"Then why are you so angry?"

He released my chin and slammed his hands on the table. "Because not only are my parents coming along to help with the dragonkin, Mother invited Briella to help!"

Now my heart did sink. "She's hawk."

Falk snorted. "Worse. She's a gryphon. The gryphons have held almost as much sway as the dragons in council, but one of theirs is the entire reason the border is back open, and it cost them at least one position on the council. Father is positive that now is the time to create an alliance with the gryphons while they are out of favor. A strong marriage would set the gryphons on the road to recovering their lost influence and help our position at the same time."

I carefully selected bacon and made myself a sandwich. "So what have you against Briella? Why not marry her? Is she ugly?"

Falk glared at me. "Do *not* join in selling me off."

I found reason to at least smile again. "I didn't say I was."

"There is no reason for you to be in favor of it."

I nodded agreeably and dared, "I'm definitely not in favor of it."

He eyed me as though expecting me to change my mind and use the opening as a way to persuade him to marry the woman. When I didn't, he said, "I have my own plans."

My heart beat a little faster. Foolish. I swallowed my bite of sandwich, refusing to meet his eyes. What would he want with a human from Anton? He was a magnificent hawk. His parents wanted him to marry a powerful gryphon. Even as he refused, his father had made it clear that a lowly Anton girl was not the next choice on the list. "I guess it is not much different here than Anton. I wasn't allowed to choose either."

"But you are here now. And I am allowed to choose." He stood abruptly and began selecting supplies. For each thing he packed, he threw one to Spark, who happily caught pieces of food midair.

"Spark! Aren't you full enough? Didn't you hunt last night?"

He peeped at me innocently.

"I know you did. The dragonsbane has long since worn off, and you never needed encouragement to feed yourself." I stood as well, crammed a few things into my own pack and eyed Spark again. "You know, someday I bet you will be large enough to carry me. Not today, but someday."

Spark squawked a happy agreement.

Chapter 16

Lindis arrived just as we finished packing up. She didn't change from dragon, and she didn't waste time with a greeting. As soon as I hopped on she took off, leaving Spark and Falk to follow.

When we reached the area where we had left Derrick and Zoe with the prisoner, we found two ogres just arriving. There was no sign of Zoe, Derrick or Vint, but Zoe had set a crystal at the base of the oak where the prisoner had been tied.

Lindis knew how to read the scrolling note inside the facets. "They saw no reason to wait," she reported. "They've taken Vint and are headed toward Typhon. Derrick is leaving us a clear trail to follow."

Follow we did. The "clear trail" was smelly enough for even me to detect, although the two ogres who accompanied us grunted and spat every time we came across a bush or rock that Derrick had marked. Lindis flew above, checking back with us periodically. Two warrior dragons flanked her each time. I was not introduced to Falk's parents or the gryphon although they flew in and around the dragon contingent.

Falk stayed grounded with me and the ogres. If being earthbound bothered him, it didn't show. He flitted in and around trees, as comfortable on the ground as he was in the sky. Perhaps he saw himself as the dragonkin saw him; merely two different guises of the same being, neither one being superior to the other.

I had never bothered to think of myself as tree, but now that I had come to know a few, the status felt more important and much more useful. It didn't make me feel less human. Maybe I felt even more human because I appreciated both forms for their advantages.

When Falk took to the sky to do some reconnaissance, both ogres slowed to walk closer, taking up positions on either side of me. If they meant to impart reassurance, they missed the mark. Either of them could crush me with the swat of one meaty, warty fist.

The one who had introduced himself as Troper asked, "Are you shifter too?"

"Me?" As if there was anyone else around to ask.

Troper grunted something in his own language at the other ogre before turning back to me. "Arto says he thinks it impolite to ask such a question, but does not know why you would refuse to answer."

I hadn't refused to answer, I'd just played dumb. Apparently the fine art of human conversation was lost on the big guys. "I'm not a shifter. I don't know whether it is impolite to ask because I am from Anton across the border." But asking probably was impolite or they wouldn't have waited until Falk had gone to do it.

The two conferred again in a series of grunts and gurgles. Troper eventually asked, "What is your purpose here?"

That was an easy one. "To help recover the dragonkin."

This seemed to satisfy Troper, but not Arto. He grunted some more. When Troper waved one giant hand in dismissal, Arto addressed me himself. "You came all this way to rescue dragonkin. This does not make sense. Your kind do not visit here often."

"Sure we do. Just not many of us." I wasn't dumb enough to implicate my uncle to two total strangers. Politics here might be foreign, but they couldn't differ that much. "I was here because of marriage negotiations when the dragonkin situation came to my attention. It must be righted." Nothing but the truth from me. I was definitely here to negotiate my way out of a marriage.

Troper nodded as though I had somehow proven his point. His big head looked as though it might roll off his shoulders like a boulder tilting precariously on the edge of a rock formation. Neither man had more than a few straggles of hair on their oversized heads. Their faces resembled boulders with boar whiskers sprouting here and there.

Troper's eyes were made small by his bulbous nose. Arto had dark chocolate skin and was perhaps an inch shorter than his companion. His nose was mashed and off-center, making his too-large eyes appear ready to squeeze out of their sockets at any moment. If he sat still, he'd look like a stone frog.

Both walked far more gently than I would have expected from such giants. They towered over me, but were careful to keep enough distance that I didn't feel truly threatened. Perhaps my imagined sense of safety was because they had ignored me up until now. Even when asking questions neither stared rudely. Their attention, like true warriors, was on our surroundings.

Arto glanced at me now. One eyeball swiveled at me while the other watched the forest in front of us. To keep up with them required that I jog periodically, but it was a comfortable manner of travel for me.

"You are small, even for a human. I do not see how you can be of any help."

I shrugged. "Probably not. But Spark is my friend, so I am determined to locate and free his parents if possible."

"You intend to negotiate with the chimera?"

Now there was an interesting idea. "No. But as you said, I am small. Perhaps no one will notice me if I sneak up to free the dragonkin while you are...pursuing other means of convincing them."

He grunted and moved back in front of me with large strides.

Falk landed soon after the conversation ended. I smiled and nodded, letting him know all was well.

"Lindis comes," he said. "She looked to be in a hurry."

It didn't take long for her to find us either. As soon as she landed, she said, "Hop on. I've found Zoe and Derrick."

She whistled at Spark and gave clipped instructions to the ogres. "Follow quickly."

Falk was already hawk and flying by the time she launched into the sky. Traveling as dragon cut what might have been nearly a whole day's walk to some steady flapping for a few minutes.

Lindis brought me up to date while she flew. "Zoe and Derrick managed to rescue a few dragonkin early this morning before light. The warriors with me will fly out with the worst of the injured. We'll get the rest out now that we won't have to waste time sneaking about in the dark."

She dropped me near Zoe and four newly released dragonkin.

Zoe sat next to one of the kin, working to release the metal locking pin. Her face and tunic were smudged with black soot.

"What happened to you?" I asked, hurrying to help.

"Got too close to one of my own explosions when a guard caught me opening a cage. There were only five guards, so we decided to rescue whichever ones we could reach. Derrick kept them busy on the other side of their camp, but the bastards got lucky and threw dragonsbane at him. I had to distract the lot of them with a crystal like the one I gave you."

I'd never had a chance to use the crystal because, as Zoe had just experienced, either I would have been too close to the explosion or the dragonkin would have been.

"Is Derrick okay?" I knew the answer because she wouldn't be sitting here if he weren't.

"The dragonsbane forced him to change, same as it did Falk, but he is a skilled fighter either way. Even though the dragonsbane is wolfsbane, he'd have to eat it for it to kill him."

"Oh. That's an encouraging thought."

I twisted and pulled on the pin, while she tapped at it with a rock. When it finally came loose, I nearly fell backwards.

"It's good you arrived when you did. Whilst Derrick was leading two of the guards on a wild goose chase, he nearly ran into reinforcements coming from Typhon."

Falk glided down, changing on the way. "Might be a good idea if you ladies herded these dragonkin to a safer place further away."

"Reinforcements?" I asked.

He looked puzzled until Zoe repeated what she had told me about the others coming from Typhon.

Falk shook his head. "The chimera approaching aren't here to join the guards. They're businessmen. One has a dragonkin on a leash, carrying packs. The entire bunch of them is armed, but it looks like they have come as buyers for more of the kin."

Zoe cursed. "That's why they had a stage! Last night when we scouted, we couldn't figure out why they had a raised platform!"

Falk nodded. "Shae—my father," he said for my benefit, "did a quick flyover. Looks like they are setting up for an auction."

"Be careful," I warned. "They already used dragonsbane on Derrick. We don't need anyone falling from the sky."

"The others know of the danger."

"I haven't figured out a way to destroy it," Zoe fretted. "We saw at least one large garden patch. We rescued the two dragonkin whose blood was being used to feed the plants, but we can't burn the stuff to destroy it because that would only endanger every shifter in the wind. We can harvest it out of there, but I don't yet know a safe way to destroy it. It's poisonous to humans too if eaten or used on the tip of a weapon."

Hmm. I wondered if I could push it underground if I turned tree. It would suffocate underground and decay. "Is it a hardy plant?"

Zoe shrugged. "Hardy enough. The gryphon's grimoire didn't waste a lot of time describing how to grow it, but it will propagate from existing roots or from seed."

Pulverized and buried very deep would likely work, but first we had other work to do.

Zoe and I urged the dragonkin further from the camp. They needed little incentive to leave, crowding close together. The stronger two helped encourage the weaker two.

Lindis had promised to bring food to help them regain their strength, but the sudden yell and crash didn't sound like her dropping in with a deer.

When I turned to look, it wasn't Lindis landing. The largest, dirtiest rat head I'd ever seen came rolling between two trees and was up and snapping at me before I could reach for the dagger in my boot.

I jumped away from a clawed paw just in time. His other half-hand, half-paw held an assassin's knife. The serrated edge glinted a deadly warning in the sunlight.

I dove right as Derrick slammed into the chimera from behind, sending both the ogre and rat heads sprawling away from me. The ogre head was much smaller than that of our two ogre friends and, oddly enough, it sported a slicked back head of hair, long past the shoulders, much like the rat head.

Zoe lifted a crystal and was ready to do serious damage, but it was over. Derrick had finished off the chimera in the roll.

"Last guard...trailed behind the businessmen." He panted as he tried to stand and move from the body. "Didn't see him...until almost too late. Drew him away rather than be discovered near camp." He sat suddenly and stared at his arm. The knife had nicked him sometime before or after the roll in the dirt. "...head...hurts."

Zoe was at his side before I could blink. "This cut isn't that bad!"

"Can't...change." His voice strained, and he frowned as though confused.

"It isn't deep enough to matter," Zoe mumbled, examining his arm. "Where else are you hurt?"

Lindis landed just ahead of us in the small clearing with the dragonkin. She was quiet about it, but she didn't have good news. "They've started burning dragonsbane," she hissed.

Zoe beckoned her over. "He breathed in some dragonsbane before, but most of it had worn off." She quickly gave details of what had just happened.

I swallowed hard and pushed one reluctant foot closer to the chimera. Derrick had twisted the knife away and used it on the assassin. He was fast, even when he wasn't wolf. But he was wolf. And susceptible to wolfsbane. And dragonsbane made from wolfsbane was the chimera's new toy.

The knife was stuck in at an odd angle. I hated rats. Miserable, dirty scrounging things. They weren't any better for sharing part of the ogre's size and head.

I studied the corpse carefully, but didn't see another knife. There was no way to know if dragonsbane had been on the blade, not now.

Derrick passed out in Zoe's arms.

"If you have a treatment for wolfsbane, start there," I advised. "That knife might have been used to harvest the stuff or maybe they decided to dip the blade in the fresh plant juices to enhance their weapons."

"They had no way to know he was wolf!" Zoe wailed.

Lindis shushed her. We weren't that far from the camp.

"If it was dragonsbane, he can't change to heal!" She was quieter now, but completely distraught.

He was unconscious, so he wasn't going to be changing anyway.

Lindis made her decision quickly. "I'm flying him out of here. The chimera have started burning the stuff for the auction. He doesn't need more of it by accident." She changed to dragon and plucked Derrick from Zoe. "Hold him on. You can both ride. We'll get him to the healer."

Lindis was a large dragon, but carrying both humans was more than a full load for her. She didn't hesitate. Neither did Zoe.

With the surprise help from one of the healthier dragonkin, we had Derrick secured across Lindis' back in short order. Zoe climbed up, her face pinched with worry.

At the last second, she withdrew a crystal from her pocket and tossed it to me. "If you can form a circle and say a word of power inside of that circle, everything inside will be deaf. It will keep the dragonkin from following orders by those outside the circle. But you have to find a way to create a circle, and I haven't time to teach you."

I handed up her pack. "Godspeed," I said, moving back to give Lindis room for take-off.

Instead of replying, Zoe's hand dug into her pack. Before Lindis had done more than stretch her wings, Zoe was rubbing salve on Derrick's wound and muttering another spell.

Lindis pushed off hard. Her wings beat furiously, holding her at nearly a standstill as she worked to gain height.

The swirl of dust and leaves left me gasping. Tears stung my eyes. Maybe they weren't all from the dust.

"Spark, can you lead the dragonkin further away?" I knew the kin understood me. They had no trouble following conversations, dragonsbane or no. "I need to stay and help. I'm the only one left who isn't affected by dragonsbane." If Falk got hit by it again...or if any of the others succumbed, there was no one left.

Spark squawked his agreement. So did the dragonkin who had just helped with Derrick. His scales were jet black, a color so deep he was a slice of darkest midnight. I touched his scales lightly, wondering if they would glow with an even sleeker ethereal darkness when he was back to full health. "You must be called Midnight. All of you, get to a safer place. And if anyone waves smoke at you, don't breathe."

There was no time to waste. I strode in the direction of the camp, stopping twice to confer silently with the forest around me. It took less concentration now, and I didn't have to change to accomplish the task, but I did find it useful to touch at least one tree. "*Are there any men near me?*"

No.

"*What of the beasts? Is there danger?*"

The trees couldn't answer such vague questions. They could identify fires, humans, squirrels—any number of specifics, but threats could be anything from a horde of beetles to a man with an ax.

I hurried on, thinking while I jogged.

I wasn't surprised when Falk landed, finishing his shift as he hit the ground. He was out of breath and sweating.

"Lindis got Derrick out," I told him.

He nodded without speaking, still gulping huge breaths of air. He put his hand out for my pack.

I handed it to him, not knowing which of the supplies he wanted. He had given me several things to keep when he went hawk. "Had to fly out of there without breathing," he finally gasped out. "We can't fly overhead any longer because of the dragonsbane."

I told him what had happened with Derrick. "They may have doused their weapons with fresh dragonsbane. If it comes to combat, you...please, be careful." I didn't dare look at him. Worry twisted my guts.

"They can't know who is shifter and who isn't, but with wolfsbane being poisonous to humans too, they probably figured it would give them an edge." Falk checked the short sword across his back and added a dagger to each ankle. "There is no reason the guard would have known to use it on him specifically. The chimera may have done the same research as Zoe and decided it's useful against a number of beasts."

"So what now?"

"The plan is to wait until the auction is over. Then we start separating the owners from the kin."

I trailed behind Falk. "Why wait?"

"The auctioneers appear to be from your side of the border. Vint definitely knew the guy, and after some pressure, told us they have a log book where they record the auction sales."

It didn't take a genius to know the value of such a book. "Which means previous sales and deals are recorded in those pages too."

"Or one like it. The camp is short at least two guards because we captured Vint and James. Derrick took out another one this morning before we arrived. The human recording the dragonkin sales has more to do than write down the details. He's also retrieving the kin, making sure they are properly drugged and turning them over to the auctioneer on the platform."

"We need that book!"

Falk nodded. "And any others like it."

The camp was nestled in a small valley below two short hills. The closer we hiked to the top of the incline, the more sounds floated up from below. At first, occasional dragonkin screams and voices broke through the trees. By the time we reached the top, it was easy to make out the bids being shouted above the murmur of the crowd.

The auctioneer's voice rose and fell as he bellowed out the finer points of the dragonkin waiting, head down, on the stage.

We were very close. I put my hand on Falk's arm. "It makes more sense for me to go closer than for you to try it," I whispered. "If they wave dragonsbane under your nose, we don't know what might happen."

"Forget it."

"Then we go together."

"Drissa—"

I held up my hand. "I'll provide cover. If something happens to you, face it, I'm the least vulnerable."

His eyes widened, and his mouth dropped as he struggled with how to point out that a girl my size was very vulnerable indeed. Every guard and chimera in the camp carried weapons. The chimera *were* weapons if you counted their rat teeth and claws. The dragonkin were under the influence and could be forced to attack me on command.

"Let's go," I said, already changing my skin to bark. The less I shifted, the better my mobility, but blending in was critical.

Falk sheathed his sword in the special harness across his back before he changed. The threads shrank into place, tightening the harness across his chest and back.

He hopped into a nearby sapling.

I checked with the trees around us in silent dryad. *"Men, other than in the camp?"* The leaves whispered amongst themselves, hesitating. *"Are there any men near us on this side of the hill? Or chimera guards?"* I tried to clarify.

Chimera and ogres.

I quickly grew more bark.

Less than a second later, a chimera guard pushed through the underbrush. Each of its heads swung a different direction; perfect for a guard.

Falk was safe so long as chimera didn't eat hawks or get the bright idea to throw dragonsbane around to test for a shifter, but the strap holding his short sword was partially visible if the chimera spotted him.

I held my breath as the guard strode by. He carried a steel-tipped staff in one rat hand. His hind feet were long and flat, easily adapted to walking. Other than a fat rat body and two heads, he could have been a furry ogre. The rat head swung around, alert and sniffing.

As soon as it passed, I followed its progress by checking with the other trees.

When the guard was far enough away, I asked about the ogres. *"There are ogres with one head? Not chimera?"*

More twittering as two oaks conferred, one quite obviously older than the other. *Only one ogre with one head. It comes with many of the slithering, but the snakes are not a danger. The ogre comes quietly, herding the snakes.*

"Snakes?" I put my hand out to get Falk's attention. It was impossible for us to communicate with him sitting so far away.

Many snakes.

"Falk." I dared not whisper louder. I snaked a branch up and tapped his wing.

He started and had to catch his balance by stretching his wings, but he finally glided down so that I could properly convey the information.

"Odd." His voice was a weird combination of a clacking human voice mixed with elongated vowels in a hiss. His hawk head tilted. "There have been rumors that snakes won't attack ogres. I know I wouldn't eat an ogre in any form. That's if you could even cut their skin. It's tougher than leather.

Mayhap snakes can't even bite it."

"Do we wait?"

"On a bunch of snakes?" He shook his head. "Let's hope they add enough confusion that we can obtain that log book."

I nodded. "Okay. But this time, perch on me. I'll see how close I can get us." I went full tree, rooting quickly. I saved most of my bulk for one long bough. Falk waited until the branch was long and bulky before he hopped along it.

I grew the limb and he hopped along its length.

The trees guided me to a spot where Falk might be able to see.

Once the branch was as far as I could extend it, I inched my roots out and tried again to walk forward.

It was an exercise in futility. Worse, I could smell dragonsbane. The sulfuric smoke was hanging in the air, even down low.

I reeled in the branch.

Not halfway back, Falk changed. Had he not been expecting it, he would have crashed to the ground.

We backed away and ducked into thick bushes.

"This can't work," I mumbled.

He was breathing hard again and held one hand against his head as if it hurt. "We can't attack until that smoke clears."

"I can get closer."

Before the argument could escalate, a twig snapped behind us.

The camp might be patrolled lightly, but there were still plenty of guards.

I hadn't realized that changing frequently was exhausting my resources until I started to add bark again. My stomach cramped and one of my legs locked up. Too bad. There were two guards batting the bushes with long spiked weapons. I didn't have time to be tired!

"You didn't hear nothing over here," a voice grumbled. "Can't hear yourself fart with all that noise from the auction."

"Saw something move, too," a different voice disagreed.

That I could believe.

Fighting these two this close to the camp was a losing proposition. I scooted next to Falk, grabbed his arm and pushed bark and tree around us both.

He tensed, his muscles as hard as if he were made of stone.

I had often wrapped my trunk around supplies, but I'd never attempted to hide another person. The sensation of building wood across the back of his shoulders was like wrapping him in a full body hug.

When I grew a leafy branch in front of his face, he finally started to relax. Maybe he feared that I would accidentally suffocate him by encasing him in wood. My leaves rustled with my giggle. Silly man. I knew he had to breathe.

"Crappers!" One of the guards yelled.

I panicked. We were so effectively wrapped in tree right now, fighting wasn't possible. With no chance to move, we did exactly nothing as a tarnished gold, brown and black snake the thickness of my leg flew overhead and smacked into the deadwood behind us. Unhurt, it slithered right back in the direction of the guards.

By now, both guards were hacking at the ground around their feet. Their rat paws and claws functioned as formidable weapons, but at least one rat head was reduced to shrill rat squeaks of panic.

"Drissa." Falk whispered, his mouth against me. His voice vibrated across my wood, echoing in my ears.

I shivered.

"I truly appreciate your affection and at any other time should you choose to wrap your body around mine, any part of your body actually, I assure you, I'd more than welcome the bounty, but could you, just this once, perhaps, free my sword arm?"

I was new at attempting to protect someone else. Simple oversight. I wasn't certain whether to be flattered by the way he phrased his question or...I couldn't have weak knees. I didn't even *have* any knees at the moment. It was just that his lips moving along the smooth oak of my skin felt oddly like a kiss.

I pulled bark and wood back, not sure exactly whether giving his arm freedom would be enough to save us. But if the man didn't want to be hugged by a tree, who was I to argue?

While Falk flipped away snakes that slithered too close, I checked with my brethren in the forest.

"Two more guards approaching," I told him. "And the ogres! They are here too!"

"Retreat might be a good idea," he muttered.

"I think we'd be more vulnerable to the snakes if we move." The idea of stomping through hordes of slithering...my mind nearly went into dormancy at the thought. No thanks.

Troper roared past us then. At least one of the guards fell flat. He was either dead or being eaten by the snakes. Troper had more than enough time to snap a huge fist into the rat face of the other guard. I didn't need to watch him complete the job; the noise was indication enough.

Wisely, I released Falk, but knew I was safer as dryad. Snakes didn't eat trees, bite trees or have any real interest in us.

Falk called out the pattern to alert Troper and Arto that we were near and friends. "What the hell is with all these snakes?" he demanded, striding over to the mess. Both guards were clearly dead.

Arto grunted. "Is normally a food source. We have ability to entice them for an easy meal. Not a skill of others, we have decided."

Good guess on his part. I certainly hadn't enticed any lately.

Troper said, "Many snakes in the area for some reason. Put them to use. Can eat later if hungry."

Falk used his sword to flick a rather large specimen away from his ankles. "Can you command them? Tell them what to attack and what to ignore?"

Troper shook his head. "Not command. Just entice. But snakes like rat bodies. Will eat the guards while we rescue the dragonkin. The kin eat snakes too so not a problem for them."

Falk might have shuddered, but he couldn't argue with the logic. "Let's get the kin freed then." He turned back to me and probably looked as though he were talking to the bushes. "You're much safer here. Wait for us."

Wait for us? Where did he think I was going to go? The forest was alive with movement. Snakes coiled up, hung from branches and slithered under and over every bush and rock in sight.

Falk flung two more away from him in rapid succession. The ogres didn't have such a problem. The snakes followed the ogres, either sniffing their ankles or nipping them, but it didn't matter either way. The ogres were obviously impervious to a mere snake bite.

"How are we going to get rid of them?" I wondered aloud.

If anyone understood the low groan of my question, none bothered to answer. Falk was already striding away, the two ogres close on his trail. Snakes by the hundreds followed.

"You're going to leave me here surrounded by snakes?" I wanted to shriek it, but being more than half tree, the question came out a low rumbling mixed with the squeak of branches rubbing together in a storm. Not that I was in any danger, not exactly, but at least four *snakes* had touched me.

I shuddered, leaves and branches protesting. "Falk!" I did not want to stay here helpless while he did battle and rescued the dragonkin. It wasn't fair. But I wasn't too keen on returning to my human shape and, I shuddered again, wading through snakes!

"Bother and damnation." Cautiously, I changed my head and arms back. When a late follower slithered by my trunk, I nearly changed back. Gritting my teeth with every ounce of determination I possessed, I forced myself to keep my eyes on the beast. It meandered calmly by, almost hypnotic in its smooth motion.

The chaos at the camp quickly turned from boisterous, competitive yelling to the deadly sounds of battle.

Would Falk remember the book? Of course he would. But in the confusion, rescuing the dragonkin had to take priority. With his sword, he was obviously the enemy. He wouldn't have time for a book.

If only I'd been able to use the crystal Zoe had given me! I could mute the commands from the slavers. The dragonkin wouldn't hear the orders, and they could escape without being forced to fight on the wrong side.

A screaming battle cry from above had me ducking back down, but it turned out to be my first close up of the gryphon. She was diving fast to avoid smoke. Her lion body was every bit as bulky as that of a dragon, but her wings were feathered. She swooped away with at least one dragonkin chasing her. She could easily outdistance it. The kin may have been told to kill her, but she was fast enough to lead it away and double back.

There was no sign of any hawks or dragons. Maybe Falk's parents had changed and gone in fighting once they saw the ogres. They couldn't get close in their hawk form yet. There was too much risk the smoke would force them to change, and falling out of the sky would be as deadly as a chimera sword or rat claw.

I uprooted myself and slung my pack across my shoulders. Maybe I could find the book. Who would notice little old me, flitting from tree to tree, half tree myself?

Chapter 17

No matter my form, I was not invisible, especially to Spark. He chirped at me as he landed nearby, now too big to even consider landing on my human form without knocking me flat. His friend Midnight was close on his tail.

"Spark! What are you doing here?"

He burbled a few dragon noises as if that would enlighten me. The smoke wasn't thick right now, but the sulfuric stink lingered and strengthened depending on which way the wind was blowing. Falk certainly wouldn't be able to risk changing to hawk. The ogres might watch his back, but even if the chimera were running flat out from the snakes, the situation was very dangerous.

"Spark, the smoke could get you killed! For that matter you could eat me for lunch if the wrong person commands you."

Both dragonkin started a cacophony of beeps and half roars that was completely lost on me. Luckily, the noise from two hundred yards away was loud enough that no one was paying attention to us.

Spark put his head under my hand, but that did nothing to help me understand. He swayed back and forth as though my hand was directing the dance. "You want me to give you commands so that no one else can? We don't know if that will work! You don't need commands, you need to go where it is safe!"

Hadn't that been what Falk told me? And was I doing what he suggested? "But rogue commands don't affect me," I muttered. I never followed orders even if I heard them.

"Wait! Not hear commands...the crystal from Zoe could make you deaf. Can you carry a crystal?" Of course he could. But I only had one. I yanked it from the pack. "If we activate this and you carry it, you won't be able to hear orders! I think. Well, she said to form a circle, and those inside would be deaf, but if that is the case, you won't be able to wander outside of the circle. And if someone came inside that circle it might break the spell. I think. I'm not a mage."

Spark squawked encouragement. Or maybe he had just proposed eating the crystal. He ate everything else.

"It might work to protect you." I followed Zoe's instructions, first circling around Spark and Midnight. I had to ensure their safety before the smoke gave anyone an advantage. Dragonkin were now flying overhead, sometimes fleeing and sometimes diving in attack. I thought I heard the gryphon again, but the screech was too far away to identify.

"Word of power. Do I say it? Or do you?" I wrapped Spark's claws around the crystal. Midnight pushed in and put his hand on the crystal too. I explained the spell again, and then activated the thing just the way Zoe had explained.

Sound ceased. Completely. Even the wind was silent. "Uh-oh." I'd accidentally made myself deaf because I held the thing while saying the word of power.

Uncertain what might happen, I pulled my hand away.

Sound! The chatter of human and rat voices rent the air again.

But was the crystal working for the dragonkin? Well, it would work so long as they both held the crystal. Probably. I was no mage, that was for sure.

"Spark? Can you hear me?"

Spark chirped. Midnight squawked. Then Spark did the most amazing and unexpected thing. He scratched the crystal with one sharp talon, cleaving it in two.

Midnight kept half.

The two of them burped at each other, but then went silent, staring at each other, communicating in that silent way of dragons.

"Okay. I think it worked. Guys, we need to retrieve a book." Only...they couldn't hear me now!

"Never mind." I slung the pack back across my shoulders and headed to the battleground.

Spark, bless his scaly hide, stayed with me. Midnight took to the air. Maybe he could give the escaping dragonkin orders to flee. Maybe he could kill a few of his captors. All I knew was that no one was going to tell him what to do. Good for him.

Only a few yards separated us from the camp. The forest around me twittered nervously about fire. More than just dragonsbane was burning now.

I changed one hand to a leafy branch and grew bark along my skin. The disguise was most likely wasted.

Spark glided ahead, watchful. If he did nothing else for me, he ate two snakes that meandered across our path.

The body of a chimera, separated from both its heads, slammed into the ground off to my side. Midnight hadn't left us after all. He flung both heads away, hissing, but not flaming. The holes in his mouth probably still hurt.

I stood from my too-late crouch. If it hadn't been for Midnight that would be my head rolling.

The auction platform was empty with the exception of one dead human and a few chimera body parts. A pit at the bottom of the platform still contained several long metal irons. The coals in the bottom burned red, but most of the smoke wasn't coming from the pit.

The fighting was mainly near the dragonkin cages now, leaving this area empty other than an occasional straggler trying to flee.

The table where the guard had sat during the auction was pushed over. No books were visible from here. I rooted next to a chalk maple bush, listening to the worried sighs of the trees. I stretched out a limb and used it to dig around the debris, but there was no book of any kind.

I'd have to get closer.

I reeled myself in and changed. Maybe Spark could hear me if I touched him. Maybe not, but it was worth a try. "Spark. I'm looking for a log book. It might tell us where the other kidnapped dragonkin are located. Watch my back."

Together, we darted out into the open. I stayed hunched, scanning the ground, but it was full of garbage; body parts, fur and blood. At the pit, I pulled one of the irons out. "Ah." The end held a metal container, much like the incense burner James had set in the coals. In this case the two irons had been left too long and all the dragonsbane had burned. I pulled the other one out anyway, and just in time.

The chimera behind me had a smoking incense burner, and he waved it freely. Two ordinary humans flanked him, either as guards or in an attempt to stay close to whoever could control the dragonkin.

Spark roared. He saved his fire, but his rumbling threat had the hair at the back of my neck standing on end.

The rat head made chittering noises, and then darted closer to Spark, waving the incense. The chimera was well-practiced in his art of slavery, using his own breath to blow smoke at Spark.

"Kill her!" the ogre head screamed, his lance pointing right at my heart.

Too bad he was lazy. Had he rushed me, I would have had been hard pressed to defend myself. By ordering the dragon to do it, he gave me a chance.

Spark, for his part, sneezed and then coughed out a flame that made it halfway up the chimera's lance. The human guards weren't as suspicious as the chimera. They held back, waiting for Spark to fall under the spell of the dragonsbane.

Even though Spark couldn't hear the commands, the poison affected him. He lifted his back leg to take a mighty swipe at the chimera, but tottered and overbalanced. His talons caught the rat head before his tail rescued him from rolling over. He went for the kill then, what was meant to be a lift-off stomp with both his rear talons, but the smoke affected his speed and accuracy. When his talons landed, they weren't all that far from the mark, but he knocked the chimera over rather than gutted it.

I'm not certain he meant to bite the screaming ogre head off, but as he struggled to breathe, he snapped and snarled. The ogre head was in the wrong place at the right time. Spark's jaws closed shut, ripping the chimera in two. He dropped the head and hissed out a protesting flame that missed the chimera completely, but flamed one of the human guards.

The other human guard rushed me, his dagger ready for the kill. I swung the metal iron fast, smacking him in the head. The force of the hit had me staggering backwards. Feeling the heat of the fire pit, I scrambled to the side, but slid and slammed into the dirt.

The guard slashed at me, swearing and yelling, "kill the woman, kill the woman!"

I rolled and slammed into one of the posts on the makeshift auction stage. "Oof." Curling into a ball, I somersaulted, flipping myself around the pole, and tucking myself under the stage.

Spark came at the guard from behind, slapping him into the stage. The man's neck hit the platform and snapped. I released my grip on the metal poker. On hands and knees, I crawled towards the other side and escape. My knee landed on something softer than the ground. My hand pressed on something smooth and moving.

Snake!

"Eeeeeeeeaiiii!" My human brain stuttered to a stop. Some part of me might have registered that the soft object under my knee was a leather bound book. Another, smarter survivalist part of me touched my dryad and changed my arm in reflex even as I screamed again. My legs tried to move forward and backwards at the same time. The snake bit down. In shock, I stared at my twig hand, wondering why the fangs didn't hurt.

Because that part of me was wood.

Spark chirped from somewhere that seemed very far away. A human face suddenly snarled in my space, a long sword swiping in my direction. My hand, a branch really, raised in self-defense, lifting the waving snake body, its jaws still clamped on my twig hand. My eyes met snake.

The shriek I let out then could have been heard in Anton. I am pretty certain my dead father heard it in his grave, God rest his soul.

I flung that snake with every ounce of tree I had in me.

It hit the human in the face.

I scrambled again, my limbs almost as drunk as Spark's. My knee slid from its perch, reminding me of the book. I grabbed for it and the poker at the same time. Crab-scurrying, I whimpered my way to the front of the platform and hit the opening at a dead run.

Snakes!

I ran. I didn't care if humans, chimera or a horde of rats shot me with arrows. Let them see if their lances could catch me.

I passed Spark without slowing down. He read my panic and left off his battle, following me in a half-flight that should have been able to catch me sooner than it did, but maybe he was still drunk on fumes. His right wing nearly took us both down as he drew even with me in a series of half hops, half-flight running.

The terrain was all uphill, but I crashed through the underbrush as though every chimera ever born was chasing and trying to kill me.

By the time I reached the top of the hill where we had spied down on the camp, my brain had slowed down enough to scan the ground carefully. I slammed my back against a protective walnut, queried in silent dryad about possible snakes and heaved air in and out.

Spark placed himself in front of me, swaying. I put one trembling hand on his neck. I was almost glad he couldn't hear me because trying to explain my panic over snakes might stretch the cultural barrier a bit thin. So far as he was concerned, snakes were merely dinner.

When nothing came at us from the direction of the camp, Spark faced me. He garbled a question.

With my hand still touching him I said, "We might be relatively safe. For the moment." There was no way for me to know if his answering squawk meant he understood. I stashed the book in my pack and then called my dryad, sending branches high in order to view the chaos below.

The tide was about to turn. Lindis had returned and organized her troops. The dragons formed a line in the sky. Their wings beat in unison and they held their place. With the wind at their backs, they flapped all the smoke in one direction out of the valley.

Briella was easy to spot. She was the only gryphon. Her muscular body was shaped with the gracefulness of a giant cat. Her wingspan was somewhat shorter than the dragons', with the feathers of her wings matching those on her elegant snow-white eagle's head. In short, she was magnificent and lethal.

The gryphon was not quite first in line, but she was close. She ripped into a line of chimera, her huge claws leaving two down and bleeding with holes where their chests had been. As her wings beat furiously, she took the head of a third guard with her. That left the body with an ogre head, but I wasn't sure if that meant it was alive or dead.

Since its rat body took aim at her with a modified crossbow, apparently it could function fine without both heads. No matter. Briella was no novice in a battle. She twisted midair and finished the job.

I tried to spot Falk or any other hawk, but bodies flew left and right. Chimera began running out the other end of the valley. Dragonkin huddled or flew aimlessly. Ordered to fight, to not fight, to flee...there was no way to discern who was screaming what.

I changed back to my human form and sank to the ground, but only after checking carefully for snakes.

Spark chirped again. I waved my hand. "Go. Help. Whatever."

He blinked, still unable to hear. I shooed him with my hands. He didn't need to be asked twice. He hardly swayed at all as he took off down the hillside.

I didn't expect Briella to have seen me run up the hill or to know where I was, but there was no missing her as she glided almost to my feet.

I was at a distinct disadvantage sitting down, but standing didn't really improve my position.

Her wings were far larger than those of a hawk and not iridescent like those of the dragons. Her face changed to human. "There's really no place for you here." Even though she had changed form, her voice was the deep purr of a satisfied cat. "He may have brought you home for the night, but you can't think it means anything when it comes to what he really needs."

I didn't like her implication of why and how I had spent the night at Falk's tree. "It would appear that his choices and preferences are up to him." My voice surprised me, channeling my grandmother when she was furious, a cross between a woman and a throaty oak.

Briella's large eyes narrowed. "You can't hope to ever be his equal. You'd be nothing more than a pretty bauble on the sidelines of his life while he tried to live out the great role intended for him."

How I wished I could hiss like Spark did. "Your thoughts on the matter are duly noted."

Briella laughed and launched herself back into the battle to prove herself to whomever was willing to watch and stand by in awe. She didn't want an equal, not even in a husband. She wanted someone she could best.

Before I could slink to a more hidden spot, another voice interrupted my thoughts. "It's good that you are willing to give in so gracefully. You are wise to admit your limitations." A woman who could only be Falk's mother addressed me from atop the deadwood Falk had used earlier. She shifted to mostly human form, her face hauntingly elegant despite luminous, watchful eyes. Silky brown hair lacked the white strands that mixed with gold on Falk's head.

Because she was perched on a branch, I was forced to look up to meet her gaze. She, like her son, was beautiful and graceful, able to claim the sky and earth as her own. Her landing in the tree was done on purpose, but I was not only used to being looked down on, I was quite tired of it as well.

She didn't know me, nor had she given me half a chance. Maybe Falk was worth all this drama, but even if he were not, the dragonkin were. I would put up with her a thousand times in order to save the dragonkin from slavery, but I didn't have to like her attitude.

"It is quite common for men to choose a wife similar to their own mother. You are both beautiful and deadly." I inclined my head in the direction Briella had flown. "I think she also enjoys getting her way and will stop at nothing to ensure it, but I suppose Falk will know how to handle being bullied constantly, don't you think?"

I turned my back on her and walked into the forest. A nearby birch rustled a warning as a squawk of outrage told me she had turned hawk. If she meant me harm, I had no defense because there was no way Falk would forgive me for even waving a dagger at her.

Before I could scoot under protective boughs, Falk was suddenly by my side.

He slapped his hand on my head just as claws raked by overhead.

I ducked, though it was too late.

"Not one hair on her head, Mother!" Falk yelled. "I swear, I will hold you responsible!"

I spun to face him. "I didn't think she'd do it." Though in truth, I hadn't cared if she did. If she drew first blood, I wouldn't have to pretend to be nice.

"Never underestimate my mother," he said with a sigh. "I thought I heard you scream." Then, looking down at me he added, "She wouldn't have done more than loose a few strands of your hair just to teach you a lesson."

"I wasn't screaming because of your mother." To avoid his gaze, I tucked my head knowing I had to confess that I'd been guilty of provoking the attack even if I hadn't started the fight. Instead, my eyes widened in shock when I saw his hand. "Your hand is bleeding!"

Huge drops of blood streamed down his fingers and dripped onto the dirt. He lifted his fingers in surprise. "Indeed. Her attack would have pulled more than a few strands. What did she say to you?" His eyes narrowed angrily. With a curse, he changed his arm into a wing, then back to fingers. It took two switches before there was little more than a pink spot because he didn't change properly on the first attempt.

"I think it's more what I said to her than what she said to me," I muttered. "Briella started it, and I wasn't keen on being told how useless I am."

"Briella accused you of being useless? Because she is able to gut a man in one swoop?"

"Two of them at one time," I pointed out.

He scanned the sky, but it remained clear of hawks and gryphons. "It is marginally possible that some men are more impressed by the saving of a life than a gutting of one."

I shrugged. "Well, it is true in this case that I am not of much use, but I didn't think your mother had to agree with her." My stomach clenched, along with my fists. "I may have implied that your mother was a bully."

I didn't dare look at him. He had gone completely still.

"My grandmother would knock my head into a tree for not being smarter about it, but I was feeling rather small and defenseless. Are all the dragonkin safe?"

He lifted his hand, studying the healing pink. "Mother is a bully, especially of late. So is my father."

I tilted my head sideways in order to peek at his face. "I shouldn't have said it anyway."

He smiled. "Probably not. But she's been convinced this was a perfect match for at least a month. She and Briella have been planning the wedding as if the two of them were best friends, and I'm just a foolish man pretending to have cold feet."

I frowned. "Does your mother really believe you'll change your mind?"

"Briella has been lying about what has been going on between us. My mother may be good at manipulation, but she seems to miss the signs when it happens to her."

I didn't have the right to ask any more questions. I barely knew this man. But I was curious. Innocent curiosity, of course. "What *is* going on between you two, then?"

"Exactly nothing. I avoid her, and have largely ignored the entire drama, which apparently was a mistake. I've had it with the lot of them," he snarled. "I would much rather have time to court you properly to set our friendship solidly, but I haven't the patience for these games." He hauled me closer by my shoulders and kissed me firmly as though that would settle everything.

He then straightened, but instead of letting me go, his hands gentled. "You are—" He blinked. "Far from useless. And beautiful besides."

I stared into his golden brown eyes, my lips too stunned to speak. My breath hadn't had a chance to catch up to the kiss or the sudden gleam in his eyes. He moved one hand to the edge of my jaw.

I breathed once more, but was still held frozen as, slowly this time, he leaned in and kissed me again, leaving me the freedom to move away or respond in kind.

Instinctively, I stepped into his protective embrace. His soft lips caressed mine. Shivers tingled up my spine until I no longer cared that the entire forest looked on or that the leaves whispered of hawks and gryphons passing overhead.

He smelled of fresh air and sunshine and tasted of apples and cinnamon. The feel of him next to me took my breath away. I had never experienced anything quite so wonderful as Falk.

He trailed his fingers along my arm to my hand. As he squeezed my fingers, he broke the kiss and leaned his forehead against mine. "Wait for me in safety. My intentions are declared."

Well, yes. I suppose they were.

Chapter 18

The dragonsbane was a problem. Even with the chimera dead or on the run, the stuff had to be destroyed. We couldn't burn it or leave it sitting there to be harvested later. If it did seed, it wouldn't be as potent against the shifters unless someone watered it with dragonkin blood, at least according to Zoe. No one really wanted to test whether or not she was right.

Harvesting the dragonsbane wasn't difficult, but it took a precise hand. We had to get all the roots, stray leaves and flower heads. The two garden plots had been well cared for, watered and blooded regularly. Pulling the roots was easy, but even a tiny leftover piece could start a plant anew. All of us used gloves because of the poison.

After bagging the stuff for what seemed like hours, I tugged Falk to the side. "Redwood, your house, could bury it."

He absently kneaded my shoulder while he considered my plan. "Redwood?"

"I thought about doing it myself, pushing it down with roots, but there is too much for me. It would take me days, probably weeks. If Grandmother were here, she could easily convince other trees to help, but I'm only a quarter dryad. Even if the forest agreed to help, they'd be sluggish about it. Grandmother has...well, she's more like Redwood. She has a lot more power."

Even though I was nearly whispering, Lindis stared my way over the heads of Zoe and Derrick. Her eyes bored into me, rather rudely. "How long would it take this Redwood?"

Zoe looked at her in surprise and then followed her focus to me.

Falk explained, "Dragons have superior hearing."

"Oh." Uncomfortable, I shifted my feet, wondering if Lindis overheard everything and what she might think of me being dryad.

She didn't waste words. "Well? How long? We aren't leaving this stuff somewhere to decay over the ages."

"I...didn't ask. Maybe a day." At her puff of impatience, I added quickly, "It could take an hour. But I won't know until I ask."

"Ask who?" Zoe put in.

Derrick crossed his arms and smiled at me. I bet wolves had pretty good hearing too. I wasn't thrilled about my secret being out, but there wasn't anything to be done about it now.

"If someone takes me there, I can ask. There isn't anyone around here who would know. Although I could send along a message, it would take time." And not even I knew if that would work because the trees didn't bend to my will like they did for Grandmother.

"It is worth consideration. I will check progress. And logistics." Lindis strode away.

Meanwhile, the one thing I did want to try on my own was to hunt out the rogue bits of root in the ground. I submerged my hand, searched around by extending questing roots and groaned. There were bits and pieces everywhere.

"Can you bury them?" I whispered to a nearby pine tree. There wasn't much wood standing in the valley; the men and chimera had cut anything useable to build cages. "Can you grow a root closer and starve them off?"

If you lend us your power, dryad.

What did that mean? And how could I possibly do that? Grandmother would know. Maybe Redwood would know too. But Redwood wasn't here. "Do you know how to borrow my power?"

Feed us.

What did that mean? Bring them water? I frowned mightily, thinking back to my lessons with Grandmother, but not coming up with anything particularly helpful. Now that I put some effort into wondering about how to ask trees for favors, I was almost certain Grandmother had been waiting for me to inquire about such a feat. Back then, using my dryad abilities had been a refuge at best and a chore at its worst. I hadn't spent any time exploring the range of abilities, namely because I had taken it for granted that Grandmother would always be able to do things I couldn't. The problem with that decision was that I hadn't pushed myself past the basics.

"What's wrong?" Falk whispered near my ear.

I jumped, flinging the wolfsbane in my hand over his head. It drifted down, looking harmless. I sighed. "Nothing."

"You're scowling. Your hand has been rooted to that spot for a while."

I retrieved my body parts and then placed the dragonsbane in one of the burlap sacks. "There are root bits left under the ground. They will sprout again."

"Weaker than before?"

I shrugged. "I don't know any more than Zoe. Without dragonkin blood they will likely be wolfsbane with an edge. I thought maybe the trees could help push the bits deeper, but I don't know how to..." I couldn't even articulate what needed to be done.

"To what?"

"To ask them. Well, I can ask them, but it's not that simple." In frustration, I yanked another plant and added it to the bag. "I need to return here sometime with Grandmother. She can help."

"Will we find her when we locate your sister?"

That made me smile. "No doubt about that. I found the book, by the way."

He froze. "You what?"

"The book of records. It's in my pack—what? Why are you staring at me like that?"

"Drissa, the dragonkin have been scouring the earth for that thing for the past two hours!"

"They are?" It had been their blood that fed the plants, and most of them were injured. Instead of helping pull dragonsbane, they had been destroying the cages and tools that had held them captive. "I thought they were just getting rid of their anger."

Falk rolled his eyes. "Lindis said it would be good therapy, but most of them know of other dragonkin that were here and were sold. They want that book as badly as we do."

"I didn't even have a chance to look at it yet. I hope it's the right one."

"Well, let's do it now. The ogres can keep harvesting. Zoe and that young dragon from Lindis' patrol have the other patch in hand."

I watched Troper pluck another root. His big hands didn't look suited to delicate harvesting, especially after I had seen those same hands squeeze the life out of the chimera.

I fidgeted. I wanted a private look at the book. Once the others got wind of it, well, there was barely a private moment now. "Okay."

My pack was never far.

The book was bent and battered. From the title etched across one side of the leather, the pages had once served a merchant. In fact, the first few pages were faded records of cloth goods, food stuffs and other trades.

After perusing several pages in, I could see we would need the help of Lindis and probably several of the dragonkin. The descriptions of the dragonkin were by size and color, but there was no mention of where they had been captured. The sale price was recorded, but the names of the chimera were often only a single name. With each of the sales, a weighed amount of dragonsbane had also been sold. In at least one case, a dragonkin sale was listed as a "blood sale." My stomach knotted.

"What do you think that means?" I pointed to the entry.

Falk glanced at my eyes, but we both knew what it meant. "They are growing this stuff elsewhere, aren't they?" I said.

"Someone has to sell it on a regular basis to those who buy the dragonkin. The slavers aren't going to hike out here every month to get a new supply. In some cases, the more ambitious owners will likely grow their own. The lazy ones will just create a market for it. If the chimera are buying on behalf of the harpies, the harpies will expect the chimera to provide the dragonsbane on demand."

"There aren't any addresses listed." My hands shook with pity at the number of slaves listed here. "It's not going to be easy tracking down the dragonkin."

Falk squeezed my fingers. "It won't be as hard as you think. The ones we've freed will be more than happy to sniff out their kin in the cities."

"What about what James said? He was planning on herding them across the border. They might not all be in nearby cities." I flipped pages looking for one name in particular.

In the background, I heard Lindis comment about people resting in the shade having lunch while others worked and patrolled. I ignored her. My hand nearly ripped the page I held. It wasn't Uncle Ralph's name on the page. It was my name. Drissa Castillo was listed as a buyer of two pounds of dragonsbane.

The notation after my name and date showed one gold piece had been paid. A second was due at Glasdon church on the fifteenth with delivery of more dragonsbane. On the margin of the page someone had scrawled the name "Ava" next to the date. "What day is it?" My voice squeaked. There was no air for my lungs.

"The tenth, why?" Falk shouldered in closer. Ava's name in the margin made it easy to see. "Your *sister* is buying dragonsbane?"

I slammed the book closed. "Don't be ridiculous! She's barely fourteen! She doesn't live in Glasdon, either! There's only one reason she'd be meeting anyone in the church there."

"Glasdon? The church on the cliff?" Lindis' voice was always cold, but it was now threaded with the promise of mayhem, a silky hiss accompanied by steam.

She had approached us quietly, her feet and hands changed to talons.

Falk was unimpressed. "You've been there?"

"Once."

"Is it hard to defend?"

She snorted. It came out a half roar. A shimmer of crimson and violet scales danced across her skin as though she were struggling to control herself. "It's on the pinnacle of a cliff, the last stand for the town of Glasdon below. It is apparently not too difficult to penetrate because Zoe and her friend managed to get inside and stop the farce of vows planned by those who stole my dragon!" She was shouting by the end of her statement, her talons flexed and ready to rend her enemy to shreds.

"Uncle Ralph is taking Ava there. To marry the prince," I whispered. Spots danced in front of my eyes.

The most amazing cursing and billowing flames burst from Lindis' fangs, causing me to instinctively suck in a deep lungful of much needed air. My vision cleared, leaving me focused on a half-changed dragon.

She might have actually burned us to a crisp had Falk not moved her way and yelled, "Control yourself, dragon! You are not a hatchling to burn down an entire forest over a past insult."

She launched herself at Falk, but he danced aside, lightly smacking her on a scaled shoulder as though they were dueling with gloves. "Enough."

Spark suddenly dove out of the sky and landed hard between me and Lindis. He roared a baby dragonkin protest, and planted himself firmly in front of me, the sharp silver spear on the end of his tail nearly cutting the log book in half. His tail was a hefty weight across my knees.

I moved his tail both to save the book and to keep from being cut to ribbons. "What insult?" I peered around Spark. It was possible no one heard me because no one answered.

Lindis still appeared ready to snap Falk's head between her mighty jaws.

She breathed hard for several tense seconds. *"Insult?"* She remained nose to nose with Falk. "Let someone take your wings from you and see if you call that a mere insult!" She poked him in the chest, her talon sharp and threatening, but controlled, if barely.

Falk gazed at her coldly, unmoved. "That is precisely what the dragonsbane did. And I don't recall roaring like a spoiled hatchling or nearly decapitating friends over it."

His words slapped her as his tap on the shoulder hadn't. Her dark skin, blacks and purples, scaled or not, paled. She stepped back. With a cough, she banked the fire that burned. After two more deep breaths, she gave him a single nod. "Understood."

After another moment, she stepped sideways to address me over Spark's bulk. "Who is this Ava?"

"My sister."

"And she intends to marry the prince of Anton?"

"Hardly." Now that it seemed safe, I found my feet. "She's fourteen. It won't even be considered legal by the king until she is sixteen, unless he changes the rules for the situation."

For a few moments I thought they might not ask, but even when angry Lindis was dangerously intelligent. My heart tried to beat its way out of my chest as her eyes narrowed.

"What might be a strong enough boon to make him change his mind and grant the marriage? Your sister is of great talent? Or riches?"

"Not really." What would they do when they saw my name as buyer? And here I was in Wendal as if I might actually be trying to acquire dragonsbane!

Falk and Lindis waited silently. Spark chirped encouragement, winding his head under my hand. That drew instant attention to the book.

Lindis looked from the leather bound copy to me. "The log book?" she surmised.

I nodded. Miserably I offered it to her.

She took it from me, but didn't open it right away.

Zoe and the ogres had stopped work to watch. The dragonkin waited patiently for the outcome.

I wished the forest could swallow me whole. She'd find the entry soon enough. "Uncle Ralph intended to offer Ava to the prince along with dragonsbane to control dragons. My name is listed in there as the buyer, but I assure you, I have no interest in dragonsbane or princes. Neither does Ava."

Lindis eyed me sharply and then paged through the book until she found Ava's name. It didn't take long.

After studying it and having plenty of time to read a few other entries she said, "Perhaps your sister aspires to control Anton. Or dragons."

I sighed. "I was the original carrot for the prince, but I escaped. My uncle must have listed me as the buyer. I didn't realize the danger to Ava when I ran..." My lips trembled. "She's not old enough to be sold." The last came out a whisper. I dared not look at Falk. If he decided I was really the buyer, I didn't want to face the accusation in his eyes.

Spark, sensing my anguish, wedged himself closer to me, facing the others. His tail wrapped around my feet. If I tried to move, I'd trip over him. Not that there was any point in fleeing. Falk always knew me even in dryad form, and the rest of them could hunt me down to the last branch anyway.

The accusation, when it came, was voiced from an unexpected quarter. "Your true colors do tell, don't they?" Briella took her place next to Falk, the sneer on her face not really detracting from her formidable beauty.

Whatever my true colors, my face flamed an angry red. Before I could reply, Falk stepped away from her and stood next to me, although he was deterred by Spark's tail. He clasped my hand. His grin was on the grim side, but he declared, "She is not guilty."

Briella snarled, "You are blinded by lust. I witnessed her running from the camp while the rest of us fought valiantly for the dragonkins' freedom. Perhaps she hides more than the log book. Her kind always do."

I gasped. How utterly rude! My outrage kept me from deciding which point to attack first.

Falk laughed. Never dropping his glare from hers, he lifted my hand to my lips. "She is not guilty."

Lindis rolled her eyes at Falk, and dismissed Briella with a wave. "Spark would not tolerate Drissa obtaining dragonsbane, now or ever. Does that dragonkin look like he's worried Drissa is about to drug and enslave him?" She pointed at Spark, who was still planted next to me, his tail wrapped protectively around me.

Briella's lip curled. "Looks to me as though she has already *used* the dragonsbane on both the hawk and the kin!" Her fists clenched. "Maybe we don't know the extent of the damage that can be done with this dangerous weed. Perhaps she has uncovered more subtle secrets."

Lindis tilted her head and glanced back at the entry in the book. "It is common for thieves and miscreants to hide behind someone else. It could be her uncle is hiding behind her. Or it could be Drissa is the one who wished to sell her sister all along." She smiled. "Of course that would mean that she had a falling out with her cohorts since they were chasing her. And she did save Falk." Her gaze locked onto Spark.

I swallowed hard, not because I feared anything Spark might tell her, but because my lungs ached, my throat ached, and I wanted to scratch Briella's eyes out. Of course, she'd swat me all the way back to Anton with one mighty swipe of a paw—or kill me with an eagle talon.

After a moment Lindis declared, "The dragonkin is free of dragonsbane." She swept Falk with her gaze. "I don't think his problem is dragonsbane either."

He raised our joined hands and kissed my fingertips again. I tugged on my hand. This was really not his fight. He squeezed my fingers. Must he...must he be so public about...even if it might save my hide?

From behind us, Derrick said, "We have the log book. The dragonsbane is loaded. Let's get it disposed of."

Briella snarled. "By her methods? Perhaps you turn yourself over to her whims too soon!"

Smoke billowed when Lindis sighed impatiently. "I will be witnessing its destruction myself, Gryphon. Even if she has ensorcelled Falk—"

"I see no magic at use here," Zoe interrupted. She had come to stand on the other side of Derrick. If a fight broke out, her hand didn't quite hide the large blue crystal tucked at the ready.

Falk may have put on *quite* the display, but he had the most loyal friends in the universe. I was touched that they stood next to me because of him. I finally squeezed his hand back, and to hell with what anyone might think.

No one moved. The wind shifted ever so slightly and the forest behind me whispered. A beautiful golden hawk took to the skies. Falk's mother, probably. I sighed. She hadn't bothered to stand by his side, and she certainly hadn't been by mine.

Arto grunted and muttered something in ogre language. Troper replied in English. "I do not understand their marriage rules either, nor have I been to this Glasdon."

Well, add me to that list.

The ogres' muttering got everyone moving. Dragonsbane was loaded onto the dragons. The kin who were healthy enough lined up to take their share.

Lindis said to me, "I'll deliver you and see to the chore." She switched to full dragon.

Before I could mount, Midnight swooped down. He glided over with his graceful kin walk and opened his talons to reveal a very small sliver of crystal.

"You shared it, I presume?" I plucked it from his hand. "Is it spent? You are no longer deaf?"

Lindis stared at him. She then looked at me. "You gave him a crystal to deafen him?" Her voice grated harsh now that she was dragon.

"Zoe gave it to me. She thought it might help protect the dragonkin. Before I went to look for the book, I activated it the way she told me to and gave it to Spark."

Lindis blinked and communicated silently with Midnight before saying, "I heard her tell you about the spell, but didn't see what good a circle of soundlessness would do. But if they can carry the spell, it could make it much safer when we are looking for the other captured dragonkin. How did you do it?"

"I followed the instructions Zoe gave me. All three of us were holding the crystal when I said the word of power. Then Spark sliced it in half."

Lindis stared at the crystal and then back at Midnight.

He looked at me then, and I had a feeling he was trying to communicate with me in dragonspeak. Apologetically I offered my hand. "I'm sorry. I can't understand you the way she does." I had to reach up to be able to rub his head. He was full-grown and though not as large as Lindis, he was still impressive.

Lindis said, "He lost his mate and dragon egg to these swine. He thanks you for his freedom. He goes with one of the groups to look for them in Typhon tomorrow."

Tears filled my eyes. "I'm sorry."

"He knows."

Midnight shifted his head, letting me fluff the scales around the spike coming out the top of his head. The spike was razor sharp on one edge, so I took great care. "Is there a chance you can find her?"

"He'll be in charge of one of the groups. The descriptions in the log book leave a lot to be desired, and there is nothing about dragons eggs being sold."

"They left Spark when he was just an egg. He hatched before they returned. Is it possible the egg is still at the nest?"

Midnight blinked a long, slow dragon blink.

Lindis shared his thoughts. "He did not see the egg taken. But didn't the thieves come back for the egg that was Spark? They would not have left Midnight's egg."

I frowned, trying to remember the sequence of events. "I think James and Vint did see the egg, but the dragonkin left their den with the egg when they tried to escape. Spark's mother had it during the fight and lost it, unless dragon eggs are usually left rolling about on rocks as they hatch?"

Lindis raised a brow. "Dragon's eggs are usually well hidden. Perhaps Midnight should detour back to the nest before heading his part of the rescue mission."

"Will you visit me when all of this is finished?" I asked him, even though I didn't know where I'd be. "Spark may not find his parents. He needs a role model." Even now, Spark was bouncing around the campsite in the hope of catching a lingering snake for the road, or in his case, the skies.

Midnight snorted. The smallest puff of smoke came out his nostrils.

"He finds you amusing."

I smiled. "Well, I'm not much of a clan, but when I find my sister Ava and Grandmother..." It was definitely "when" and not "if." I just had to hurry. Even if Ava were somehow married to the prince, I would rescue her.

Midnight raised a wing at me and then backed up to launch himself away.

I boarded my own flight, and Lindis headed for Falk's tree.

Chapter 19

As soon as Lindis set me down, I told Redwood what had happened, and described how I hoped he could bury the dragonsbane safely. The other dragons waited, circling above us.

Where the light entered, behind and beyond my trunk.

Hiking around Redwood was not difficult, but I had to root twice to obtain specific directions. Further from his trunk than I would have expected, a large twisting of roots held the soil at bay. Dark earth waited far below.

I listened carefully, but there was no sound of water. Out of curiosity, I breathed deeply, my dryad finding the water, but not where I expected it. This was not the same opening as the one I had seen from the cavern.

"Okay," I told Lindis. "Drop it all in here. Redwood will take care of it."

"It cannot be allowed to grow again, be used, be burned or root."

"He knows. It will go deep and decay."

Spark didn't wait for permission. He had flown with one of the smallest bags of roots. Down it went.

The other dragons, one by one, dropped their burdens.

"That is all." I looked at Falk. He nodded.

I ushered Lindis and Spark away, feeling Redwood move even as we hiked back to the front of the house.

"I do not love this solution." Lindis paced back and forth. "Would that we could burn it and know it was gone."

"It is gone," I assured her "If you circle back and search, there will be no sign of the opening. No one will find it even if they dig."

Lindis stared at me. Maybe she even read my mind.

Instead of following us inside, she stomped back around the side of Redwood.

Peering after her, I asked Falk, "Can I go down into the cavern and check on progress? I don't think Redwood is going to invite Lindis to go below and oversee operations. I can give her an update, but I wasn't about to jump in after the dragonsbane. There is suspicion on me as it is. Someone might have decided I was going to hoard and steal the lot of it."

He grinned. "The dragons know better, as do I."

"Well, there is no point in giving anyone more ammunition."

"Make yourself at home." He brushed a stray lock of hair away from my face, letting his thumb caress my cheek. "I'll cook dinner."

I held my breath. He was so compelling. And just...so Falk.

There might have been other doors leading below, but since I didn't know how else to get down to the cavern other than through the bathroom, that's the route I took.

I washed up a bit and realized my clothes were a hopeless mess again. I needed a shower and a change of clothes. At least I still had a clean chemise, but the leathers needed a good washing.

Before I could request an entrance, Redwood opened the door back out to the living area. Knowing it wasn't worth arguing, I sighed.

Lindis was there and full of complaints. "I could not find it. There are no roots winding wide like before. The soil is undisturbed. What roots I found had moss covering them. They have not moved since ancient times."

"It is buried," I agreed.

"How far would I have to dig to find it?"

I put my hand on Redwood, but wasn't really looking for answers. "You would never find it. The soil would fill in, the roots would stymie you." I shook my head. "It is truly gone in a way that I could not accomplish unless I stayed tree for long enough to wait for the decay. Redwood isn't going anywhere so neither is the dragonsbane."

She scanned the spiral staircase leading to what was probably a bedroom. "Even if this tree were burned or chopped down?"

My mouth gaped wide with the horror of such an idea. I flinched away from Redwood expecting a blast of anger, but he merely laughed.

"I don't think it would be a good idea to try that. But it wouldn't matter. Even if Redwood were..." I would not say it. "The dragonsbane is gone."

Lindis waved a hand at the warm flat bread Falk offered her.

I was too hungry to turn it down. Inside the flat bread, grilled meat, although cold, tasted wonderful. He set out grapes and cheese.

"Can you dig it back up, human tree?" Her voice was cold, but lacked her worst threatening tone.

I put my hand flat on the table and asked in silent dryad, "*If I wanted the dragonsbane back, and you decided to give it to me, could I get it back?*"

It is buried and being buried deeper as we speak. It is possible if you could convince me of the worth of the idea, but it would be wrapped well in soil and stone.

"*How long before it is but dirt?*"

It loses itself to bits even now.

I shook my head at Lindis. "It's possible for the next few hours that if Redwood were convinced of the need, we might be able to get some dirty limp pieces. But it is already buried. It will decay under the dark and pressure of the earth."

She gave a short nod. To Falk, she said, "See to her safety and that of the dragonkin. Spark will join us in the morning in the hunt for the remaining enslaved kin."

I frowned. "He decided that or you did?"

"I do not coerce any dragon or dragonkin. He has a duty. He is dragon. He will see to it." She looked at Falk. "See to yours."

Without another word, she stalked to the door and took her leave.

"She doesn't believe me about the dragonsbane, does she?"

Falk talked with his mouth partly full. "She does or she wouldn't leave. But she's letting me know that if she is wrong, I'm still responsible."

I frowned. "I'm not sure I follow that logic. Or like it."

He shrugged. "She is dragon. By their nature they hold power, and they dole out responsibility as if they rule all of Wendal, even though we rule ourselves. She is treating me as she would a dragon, which means she considers me her equal." He shrugged, but looked pleased. "She wanted to make sure that I knew that she will blame me if anything goes wrong."

I stared at him. "And that doesn't bother you? What if I am really guilty of...of something!"

"Are you?"

"No! But she can't just hold you responsible for someone else!"

"She is dragon. They do things like that all the time. We generally ignore them, but much of the time we side with them because they generally use their strength over others when something has gone badly wrong."

"Like with the dragonkin?"

He nodded, still eating.

It took me a while to resume my meal, but I was very hungry. "By responsible...she means she would make you fix it?"

He smiled, his eyes glinting amusement. He erased any doubt of what she meant. "She is promising punishment, fix it or not. That is the dragon way. She could make a refugee out of me if she chose."

I sighed. "Well, at least in this case you have nothing to worry about."

As soon as we had eaten our fill, I headed back to the bathroom.

This time, Redwood opened the door leading down into the cavern. I took the stairs two at a time. Somehow, Spark had beat me there. He was busy watching the last of the burlap disappear under roots and soil in a part of the cavern that hadn't been visible before.

The babbling of the stream was loud down here. Bits of dying daylight shone through from above, but not directly over the churned soil. Thinking to take another drink, I leaned near the pool of water. Spark breathed deep and belched a huge flame into the water.

I yanked my hand back, but not before I realized he was heating the water. "Now, how did you know I wanted a hot bath?"

Spark did his trick again, warming the water more. I grabbed soap from my pack and jumped in, leathers and all. Spark joined me, and I realized the hot bath was for him, not me.

I laughed. "You probably were just as dirty as me, weren't you?"

I scrubbed, stripped, scrubbed again and floated until I nearly fell asleep and drowned. Lethargic and tired, I hung my leathers and found my clean chemise.

Spark heated the water again, just in time for Falk, although since the dragonkin didn't follow me out of the pool, it was still probably for his own comfort.

The light had faded now. Falk was little more than a shadow, and Spark was a lurking monster splashing about in the water.

"I brought some more food down," Falk said. "It's on the moss. Do you need a light?"

"No, I can find it."

I was too exhausted to eat much more. After one grape and a bit of cheese, I lay down on the fluffy moss. Falk had provided two down pillows. I guess when you're hawk, there are lots of extra feathers to be put to good use.

I dozed, listening to the splashing in the dark. Spark flamed a time or two, once in the direction of the hanging leathers.

I lost track of time then, caught in a half-dream state listening to the earth, the water and the creaking of Redwood.

Falk whispered in my ear, "I do have a bed, you know."

My heart tripped over itself. "I..." I blinked, but it was very dark now.

He laughed and pulled me close. "I brought a blanket." He pulled the blanket across us. "You are safe with me, Drissa."

I was the tiniest bit apprehensive, it was true. Still, when he put his arm around me, I couldn't resist snuggling against his chest. Now he could feel my heartbeat, my insecurity and nerves. Maybe I wouldn't be able to sleep at all, not this close to him.

Spark peeped and curled up nearby.

I stared into the dark, smelling the lovely water and the freshly turned soil. By now, the dragonsbane was gone, buried where prying eyes would never find it. I spread my fingers, meaning to touch Redwood under the moss, but instead my hand curled around Falk's forearm.

I'd ask Redwood about it later.

I drifted into dreams of floating in a warm pool and flying in the sky on the back of a white-winged hawk.

Chapter 20

I awoke to kisses on the back of my neck. Oh...my. A warm, strong hand rested on my hip, occasionally kneading my waist. I had never felt quite so awake in all my twenty years. I didn't know whether to move or stay frozen; I was restless and perfectly content at the same time.

The cavern was still dim, but gentle shadows rested in the corners now, rather than pitch black darkness.

Falk's hand trailed down my thigh, the sensation giving me absolutely no reason to protest. My sigh was cut into pieces as my breath hitched. Feeling the length of him against me convinced me to turn, my heart fluttering. I kissed his neck even as he kissed mine.

His mother is pounding on the door above.

I honestly did not care. My focus was saved for Falk's lips caresseing my jaw, my neck and my shoulder. I dared run my fingers down his arm and moved my leg the tiniest bit over his. When he didn't protest, I scooted closer still.

Should I allow her in?

It took a moment for my brain to register the question. "What*?!?*" I sat up abruptly. "Are you crazy!?! Don't you dare!"

Falk sat up nearly as quickly. He stared at me, his breathing uneven. "My...apologies. I quite... forgot myself in the moment."

"Not you!" I struggled to get my own breathing under control.

"Pray tell, who the hell did you think it was?"

"What?"

His voice dropped to a dangerous growl. "Just who were you expecting to find in your bed this morning?"

"Who? My...No one!" I stuttered. "I wasn't talking to you. It's your mother. She's upstairs knocking on the door, and Redwood wants to know if he should let her in. Normally, he knows you bid her welcome and I...oh, good Lord. I do not want her to come in and find...and...as you can imagine..." I stumbled to my feet. "I'm not even dressed! I wonder if my leathers are dry."

The first step I took placed my foot right on Spark's tail. He beeped a protest. I yelped and jumped back, knocking into Falk, who had gotten up behind me.

His arm caught me around the waist, but my momentum took us both backwards.

We landed right back in nearly the same compromising position where we had started, his hard body under mine. I sat, stunned. Neither of us was fully clothed and even if we were... "Did you let her in?" I demanded, putting my hand on the moss, speaking both aloud and in dryad.

I thought it best to wait for your answer.

"Well, then don't. Falk can let her in when we get upstairs. Right?" I turned my head, nearly knocking him in the nose. "Is that okay?"

Falk rested his lips against my neck. He chuckled, shifting slightly underneath me, letting me know he'd be happy to stay right here. "Whatever you say."

I struggled to my feet. If there was a proper protocol for this situation, Grandmother had not deemed it necessary to teach me. I was finding a few gaps in my education lately. Of course, even if she appeared at the door today, I was not asking her for advice about this particular problem!

My clothes were dry enough. By the time I was dressed, Falk had disappeared up the stairs, no doubt intent on opening the door before his mother attempted to break it down.

My face flamed. "Goodness. With the delay she'll assume the worst."

Or perhaps the best.

I had no reply for that. I gathered my things and took to the stairs, Spark close on my heels.

By the time I puffed my way into the kitchen, Falk was alone. Smiling.

"She brought breakfast. Didn't say anything."

"Does she always bring you breakfast?"

"Generally only as appeasement. Hungry?"

"I suppose. I need to get to Glasdon."

He nodded, handing me a cup of warm milk. "We'll go."

"Falk, I know you promised to help, but I can't ask you to—"

"We have time to reach Glasdon easily before the date in the log. Otherwise, Lindis would likely put off her part of hunting the rest of the dragonkin to get you there on time."

Spark scooted by me to the outer door. I opened it for him so he could forage for breakfast before dawn made it to sunrise. Well, the sun was peeking out in red and pink already. Not that the time of day seemed to matter to him. He ate at all hours and if not snoozing, he hunted constantly.

"This might not be the safest journey to take," I confessed, quite miserable.

Falk glared at me. I sighed and drank my milk.

"Your mother doesn't like me, you know."

Falk shrugged and continued buttering his toasted bread. "You did her a favor calling Briella into the open. She and Father both heard her attack you over the log book."

"None of that made me look good, either!"

"Not your fault. The mess was not of your own doing. We hawks pride ourselves on studying the lay of the land. They could see the same evidence Lindis pointed out. And honestly, I don't think Mother cares who I choose so long as I choose soon."

I frowned. Being a convenience was not a high compliment.

Falk laughed. "No one will decide other than me." He chewed and swallowed before adding, "And you."

We finished breakfast quickly with Falk storing much of it for later and packing the rest to take with us.

My pack was still ready to go so I studied the maps. Falk added Glasdon to the leather he had provided. "Traveling fast, we can get there in a couple of days. I'll scout ahead periodically and travel with you otherwise."

Spark joined us as soon as we stepped outside. His greeting was more of a "meeeep" than his usual happy chirp. His head was down, and he was one sad dragonkin. His scales weren't dull like they had been from the dragonsbane, but he rested his head on my shoulder, his big eyes as sad as my own.

"Time to go, dragon?" I tried to be brave for both of us. "Did you eat enough breakfast?"

He puffed out a heavy sigh, his brimstone breath enough to knock me backwards.

I coughed and turned my head for fresh air. "Well, I know, there is never enough food, is there?" I rubbed his scales and, throwing caution to the wind, hugged his neck tightly. "Don't forget how to use the crystals! And we'll meet back here as soon as we're done, right?"

Spark had always understood me better than I understood him, but this time we were in complete agreement. He gave another long mournful meep, puffed smoke, and in true dragon fashion waddled away gracefully to where he could takeoff.

He gave me one last look and a lifted wing.

I waved and sniffled. Before I could look even more like an emotional nitwit, I quickly extracted the map from my belt, pretending to need a last check. A tear fell and left a disgraceful blotched mark.

Falk ignored the display. He bade Redwood to give no one entrance unless it was an emergency or Redwood deemed them worthy. "You know the list," he said.

There was so much I wanted to ask Redwood, but there wasn't time. There were far too many holes in my education. I whispered a quick, "Thank you," and told him I needed to learn how to ask the forest for more help, explaining that a tree had revealed there was a way to share my energy.

It can be dangerous, dryad. Your power is but kindling now, although it is growing. If you need help, it is better to ask and hope the forest spirits are strong enough to respond.

I gave Redwood a final pat and followed Falk.

Traveling with Falk was infinitely easier than traveling alone. We set a quick pace; I was used to half jogging much of the day, and Falk was every bit as competent. His knowledge of local trails came in handy. Our progress was efficient because we didn't have to fight the underbrush.

"There are better roads, but it's best to avoid them. I'm not as familiar with trails near the border, but I've seen some from the air."

As soon as Falk finished the second scouting, he asked about my uncle.

"It's a tangled story," I confessed. "My father was a loyal governor to the King of Anton, but upon his death the king refused to grant that title to my uncle. Titles are doled out as favors, and Uncle had no leverage. His idea of playing politics usually involved buying officials with someone else's money."

"A truly delightful relative."

"If only we had a normal black sheep to keep stuffed in a castle where he could do no harm. When Father died, neither Ava nor myself were of age to control our inheritance. Grandmother planned to raise us, but Uncle Ralph, the rat, petitioned the king and was granted permission to adopt us. He did it solely to gain access to our supposed fortunes, but Father had made certain Grandmother controlled most of it in case of his death. Uncle has been on the warpath against us since."

"Your grandmother stayed to raise you?"

I smiled. "Exactly. But as soon as I turned seventeen, Uncle began plotting to give me to the highest bidder for his own gain. I've been evading marriage arrangements easily because most officials have no desire to tie themselves to someone whose monies are unknown and controlled by my grandmother.

"Grandmother would have kidnapped us both away long before now, but if she gave us any monies or put any property in our name while we were underage, Uncle would have siphoned it off. On my birthday, Grandmother made certain I controlled my share, but Uncle was still legally in charge of Ava."

"It needs to be asked, how was your grandmother safe from him? If you are her only heirs, wasn't she in imminent danger?"

I nodded, touched by his hesitation and quick grasp of the difficult situation. "Yes. But Uncle Ralph doesn't know just how much Grandmother controls, nor does he know how to obtain the money if she dies. In the beginning, he thought he'd find out and be rid of her, but Father and Grandmother were quite clever. None of the property is in one place. The gold and silver, well, Grandmother is a dryad. It is where only she can reach it. And now, I suppose, I can too."

Falk slowed slightly. "Did he never use either of you to blackmail her?"

"Of course. And we didn't always win, either. Grandmother has been paying for everything for some time. She did refuse to pay his property taxes last year, which was one of the rare recent wins, but then, of course, she overheard that Uncle had negotiated a deal to marry me off to the prince in exchange for a title and lands. I'm guessing the king would get dragonsbane and probably a dragonkin as well."

"And a dryad. You have long needed a champion."

"Or an assassin," I muttered.

His eyes glinted with approval. "Was that not possible?"

"It was possible. It was a route we opted not to take. Instead, when the latest battle over taxes happened, I hid where I wasn't likely to be found. Ava was also well concealed nearby. The tax was already late. It was pay or lose the castle. It's a modest property, but the only thing in his name. Grandmother had no fear of being thrown out. She could live in the forest for years and in fact, prefers it."

We walked for some time before the path widened. Traveling side-by-side was more convenient, and more than that, pleasant.

"Politics in Wendal are not quite so cutthroat, at least not in my family," he said. "Despite the recent fits by my mother and father, neither would force me to marry."

"Or try to steal your inheritance, your home or that of your brother or sister."

"I only have one brother."

"I should like to meet him someday," I said. "When Father was alive, we were a family. I've tried to protect Ava as much as possible, and really the last year was the worst. So long as Grandmother provided for Uncle's whims now and then, the burden was mostly on her."

"Ah, but free of you, life would not be the easier for her."

I smiled wanly. "That is what she told me when I found her in tears one time. She had lost a battle with Uncle. His demands escalated over the years. This last arrangement..." I turned my face away and continued. "The prince has been rumored to be ready for marriage two or three times; apparently Uncle finally believed he had just the thing to sell. By myself, I would not be enough of a lure, but dragonsbane? And after the prince had been captured by dragons." I shook my head, still not believing the gall. "I can imagine the king and the prince want some way to fight back or at least the appearance of standing a chance."

Falk chuckled. "The prince wasn't captured by dragons. He was kidnapped by his own people with some grand plan they'd force him to marry Lindis to form an alliance with the dragons. That is why Lindis blows steam out her ears any time it's mentioned. They kidnapped her too. Had Zoe not come to the rescue, there would have been some surprised people in Anton when it turned out that Lindis is not to be messed with whether in dragon form or not."

"The rumors were confusing at best."

We ate lunch walking. I would probably have continued the journey well past dusk because of my hurry to arrive at Glasdon, but Falk was more patient. "Better to be rested and ready when we arrive. We still have three days."

"If the date is correct. Uncle Ralph is more than happy to tell one person one thing and another something else," I fretted. There was no denying we were making good time though.

Falk provided grilled rabbit for dinner. With our supplies it was a veritable feast.

Because it was safer and more comfortable, I decided to go dryad for the night. As I grew roots, I hesitated. "Falk?"

"What?"

I couldn't see the expression on his face now that he had banked the fire. "How did you know it was me that first time after I ran away from Derrick's cottage? I should fix whatever I'm doing wrong. Little details could be important someday if I need to hide."

He cast aside the stick he was using to poke at the coals and faced me. He might have been grinning. He held my shoulders gently and leaned in to kiss me, a gentle quick brush of his lips against mine that, for a moment, threatened to linger. He pulled back and said, "I like my original answer. You can't hide your beauty from me."

When I groaned, he laughed. "You might be right. Redwood and your grandmother would probably insist that you should know."

"So? What am I doing wrong?"

"Nothing. And maybe no one else would notice, but I was hawk. When I inspected the other trees nearby for clues, I noticed ants on one and a beetle on another. There were bugs all over."

I sucked in a surprised breath. "But not on me! That's why you were hopping all over, and I was worried you might peck me to death with your sharp beak!"

"I never once hurt you!"

"No, you did not. But then you began flirting—"

"Flirting? How does a hawk flirt with a tree?"

"Don't you dare deny it!" I poked him in the chest. "You knew, and you were letting me know and—" I wasn't going to tell him that his dance across my branches had sent shivers all the way to my toes.

He moved one hand to the back of my neck and kissed me again, renewing all the shivers and eliciting a different kind of groan.

"You're even beautiful when you're angry," he whispered in my ear.

"I'm not angry." My breathing was a bit uneven, but it was definitely not because of anger. "I'm changing now, and do not put ants all over me! I'll figure out an answer to that problem later."

He chuckled. "I wouldn't dream of doing any such thing. Besides, I'll be guarding you tonight. You're safe with me."

In some ways, yes. In others, not exactly, and he knew it too.

Chapter 21

Morning was a rude awakening. A large elm whispered a warning. It would have imparted news of the riders even had I not asked the trees around us to inform me of anything passing through because a large number of travelers was unusual here.

Men. Horses. They move with stealth.

I startled awake, too disoriented to ask questions right away. *"How many? Which directions?"*

All directions. You are the center.

I changed enough to speak. "Falk! Horses and riders coming!" The moon was still more visible than not, but the gray sky had lost its deep nighttime black.

Falk glided to a different tree.

With dread in my heart, I asked the question that had to be asked. We were too close to Glasdon to ignore the possibility of my uncle lurking. *"Do any of the riders wear an emblem of fire and ax?"* Shortly after Father's death, Uncle Ralph had applied for the crest. The king, perhaps feeling a boon would suffice in place of not passing along the governorship, granted it. Uncle took great pleasure in owning a crest that was a direct threat to Grandmother.

It took far too long for the trees to decide because pictures of things were not the same as actual things to them. I peppered them with other questions, easier ones.

They answered the easiest ones first. *No ogres about. No dragonkin, but one prisoner is bound by ties. There is a man with a hat made of pounded metals. He carries an ax strapped to the back of the horse.*

Uncle's stupid kettle hat was supposedly spelled to deflect an entire tree if one were to fall on him. Sadly, Grandmother had never tested it. His full crest of ax and fire was etched into the hat, but the trees did not associate drawn flames with the real thing.

As soon as I gleaned every possible hint from my friends, I went full human. "It's my uncle! The trees report several horses. Riding in from all directions as if they know where we are."

"Stay here." Falk took to the skies.

I didn't know whether to be dryad or human. Falk couldn't ambush all the riders from above even if they weren't expecting him.

His piercing scream of outrage cut through the morning, only to be suddenly silenced.

I searched the heavens, fearing an arrow. It was worse. The blood to my pounding heart froze as surely as his battle cry. A huge gryphon had swooped low and fast as though she had been waiting for this moment, knowing he'd go hawk.

Briella's eagle talons clamped around him tighter than leather binding.

"Falk!" It came out a pained whisper, although my stealth was wasted.

My uncles minions were corralling me. It could be no one else because no one else would bother. But...what did Briella have to do with him? Had Briella simply followed us and waited for an opportune moment?

I changed to dryad, watching Briella's wings beat hard to gain altitude. With a cry of triumph, she banked hard right and flew off.

"Bitch." There wasn't time for muttered oaths, but if I ever caught her in human form, I'd beat her with a stick so soundly, she wouldn't dream of running off with my...with my...with anyone I knew.

If Briella thought kidnapping Falk was the best way to win him over, she was in for a big surprise. If she let him loose for even a second...oh, the situation was hopeless indeed! As gryphon she was larger than Falk, had more weapons, and since she flew off with him, the location would probably benefit her as well. Falk would have to make up for those things in cunning and smarts. She was obviously short both of those if she thought the way to a happy marriage was force.

If my uncle was somehow behind this entire disaster...Well, I'd kill the prince before I'd marry him. More pertinent, I'd kill my uncle before I allowed myself to be turned over like a pig to slaughter. "I escaped you once, Uncle. Nothing will stop me from doing so again. Self-centered, ignorant, bastard criminal."

I had not yet learned to walk as dryad, but that did not stop me from trying. Root by root, I inched away from the camp. I'd sneak right through those horses and let them surround empty forest.

The light was still low morning, giving me a little time to hide. Bark and leaves became my arms and face, but the rest of me remained human. Progress was still awkward. The two packs weighed me down, but I was not about to leave them extra supplies or any proof of our stay.

The first rider was noisy enough that I had plenty of time to fully change.

He carried a crystal lantern, held high. "They were here! The hawk is gone, as we agreed."

As who agreed, you monster?

My uncle came crashing through the brush, cursing. "I'd no intention of letting that gryphon escape, whether she really led us to them or not. Damn. I thought surely she would land and then we'd have an edge over her."

Briella had sold us out? But...all to kidnap Falk? She *had* overheard my need to go to Glasdon. Everyone had heard the story when we found the book. She had even heard my uncle's name. My travel plans, including Falk's intention to accompany me, would not have been hard to assume. Had she found Uncle, cut a deal and then followed us?

"Drissa! My darling niece! We know you are here." Uncle chuckled, quite pleased with himself.

My lips curled even in bark form. By lengthening my trunk just a little bit, the glen was visible. I hadn't covered much ground in my attempted escape.

My uncle was as pompous as ever. Even out on a mission, he was dressed a cut above the rest, his shirt tailored with cuffs and collars. His black beard was trimmed as though he were about to present to court. His kettle helmet was polished and gleaming.

Two guards were with him in the glen. From the noises and snorting of horses, several others were beating the underbrush. Behind Uncle's mount, slumped over a horse, and tied to within an inch of being able to breath...Grandmother! No one else had quite that mix of black, gray and white hair falling every which way, some curled, some straight up and all of it dear to me.

Uncle combed his mustache with one gloved hand, as though considering his options carefully. "We've brought you a present! Your grandmother missed you terribly. And just for you, I'll set her free as soon as you show yourself. Come now, dear girl. Don't make me wait!"

My insides churned. Why hadn't Grandmother warned me? Why hadn't the trees told me? I knew her dryad better than my own!

There was nothing in the trees to tell me she was near. There was no strong presence...but wait. There was an odd murky empty spot, like a hidden cave. It almost smelled of her. Was it her? But how could it feel so distant if she was right here?

In dryad I demanded of the trees, *"Do you see the other dryad? The stronger one?"*

The trees whispered, but had no answers.

Was she dying? Or was she just not there the way I expected? Had Uncle drugged her? How else could he have gotten the upper hand and forced her here?

I could sense her, but it was as if her dryad was gone or hidden behind a veil.

"Well, Drissa, I am sorely disappointed. Have you not missed your dear uncle? I only mean the best for you." He chuckled again and to my utter dismay, he reached into a side pocket and withdrew, of all damned and bastard devices, an incense burner.

But the dragonsbane didn't work on dryads. At least it hadn't worked on me. Had he used it on Grandmother? Did it work differently because she was full dryad and I only a quarter?

If dragonsbane was keeping her bound, perhaps there was a way free of this after all. I wished now that I had stayed closer, but I had played this game before. Speed was of the essence. Uncle was not a patient man at the best of times.

I snaked a root out as I had done when rescuing the dragonkin, my knife wound tightly at the end. The sun was up now, but with no one staring directly at me, it was safe to shrink myself and use my bulk to grow closer. Walking had, once again, proven a waste of time.

"For every minute you delay, I will chop down one of these fine trees." There was a sound of shifting and weapons drawn from leather. "And for every minute, I'll carve a finger from your grandmother. Do you imagine she will grow her digits back? I wonder if they will come in crooked like a tree trying to regrow?"

I had to get closer. If he went near Grandmother, he would spot the suspicious root sawing away at her bonds.

"Make my words bounce," I begged the trees. *"The men are dangerous. Help me!"*

One by one, the trees drew their branches down, much as when Grandmother commanded them. I was not fooled. They had heard Uncle's threat. It served them well and whether they drew on their own power, mine or Grandmother's didn't matter.

To distract the men, I shouted loud. "Nooooo!"

The trees had heard my plea, and they responded, bouncing my protest from trunk to trunk. Branches creaked. Leaves rustled with invisible wind.

The men on horseback muttered uneasily, turning back and forth to find the source of the noise. The one closest behind me stopped, maybe frozen in fear.

I pulled myself in and dared two risky strides forward, already winding my root with the knife closer to Grandmother before taking full tree form again. The scene had not improved. Uncle was still mounted, shifting, listening.

"She is here. Chop." His hand went down, but of course, he would not do the work himself.

One of the men dismounted and strode for the nearest tree, the elm that had warned me.

The tree screamed as the ax bit into wood.

I carved at the ropes that bound Grandmother to the horse. She might fall off, but even that would cause a delay. The saddle protected the horse from my awkward cutting, but when I tried to saw the rope binding her wrists, blood dripped. I pushed one thin root under the rope hoping to cut myself rather than her as I sawed at the ties.

As soon as we touched flesh to tree, her dryad warned in my head, "Do not breathe the smoke!"

"Grandmother! How do I fix this? Are you compelled to do as he asks?"

"Whatever gave you that idea? Would I be tied like a lamb for slaughter if I walked around obeying a word that jackal uttered? He has stolen my dryad, but he will never command me!"

That was something at least. Her warning was well-timed too, although I wouldn't have needed it. I had seen what the dragonsbane did to the dragonkin. I knew what to expect from the incense burners.

"Come along, Drissa. Come along." Uncle's attempt at singing was woefully short on melody.

I kept working at the ropes, longing to shut out the screaming of the dying tree. With every chop, my own limbs trembled. I needed hands!

Uncle circled the glen, wafting smoke everywhere. The only boon was that he paid no attention to Grandmother at all.

I withdrew my roots, keeping only a trunk and the one long limb to Grandmother. I uprooted and fell sideways, nothing but a fallen log now, one that protected two packs hidden inside. From the ground, there was less danger of the smoke reaching me, but from the ground I could not see well at all.

One of the men on horseback shouted, "Here!"

He must have seen me topple because the next thing I knew, a boot was planted firmly on my trunk and the odious man was claiming victory.

Uncle stormed over, ready with the dragonsbane. As tree I could breathe through my very skin and leaves. Timing was critical. There was no point in waiting.

My mouth and nose formed along the ground, even as I stuffed the knife into Grandmother's hands. "Cut yourself free. Hurry!"

All of me had to be close in order to time the shift to my benefit. I snaked the last root home.

The smell of the smoke was just as bloody as the dragonsbane from before, but there was a deeper woodsy scent to it as well. Perhaps it was the dirt I smelled. I shifted again, more to one side to avoid the fumes.

Finally, all of me was close enough. With rage and regret, I shifted to human, holding my breath.

Chapter 22

Falk considered shifting human to make it more difficult for Briella to carry him, but the wench cared for no one more than she did herself. If the task became too onerous, she might very well allow him to tumble to the ground and die, despite the trouble she had gone through to kidnap him.

He screamed a challenge that carried across the sky, freezing animals below and alerting every other raptor of danger. He would force her to release him while he was hawk.

His claws and wings were pinned under her talons, but his beak tore a nice bloody gash in her foot. *First blood.* He stabbed and ripped again before her bellow of pain finished echoing across the horizon.

With another slam of his beak, he cracked bone. Her talons spasmed with the pain, and he twisted, trying to squeeze free.

She clenched her claws as if she were killing prey.

No matter. If he succeeded in cutting off part of her foot, it wouldn't grow back regardless of how many times she shifted.

His next strike tore higher into her leg.

She was not helpless. After the initial surprise, she retaliated by drawing her claws tighter. Her giant talons drew blood and air became hard to come by, but Falk only fought harder.

He demanded his freedom.

Hammering and twisting, he was rewarded with the sound of another bone cracking, but by then his hawk vision was fading to black. Was it her foot that snapped or his own wing breaking under the force of her claws as she fought to immobilize him?

No matter. *You will release me, and your death would be too kind an ending.*

* * *

I pulled in my stomach and pushed out my chest before reversing the illusion of breathing. Let Uncle think I was inhaling his poisonous smoke. Only...that scent! It was all Grandmother, so precious to me.

A moment of confusion nearly had me in a panic. Wasn't I going to remain part tree and breathe low? I...could not...remember!

The sweet scent of Grandmother, a woodsy smell of home and comfort, beckoned me. I closed my eyes against sudden tears of longing. For the first time, I truly understood why Spark had hurried to get closer to the smoke. Maybe the dragonsbane remind him of his own parents or the safety of his nest.

My lungs ached for air, and my heart hurt with the need to inhale the comfort of everything good in this world. Grandmother would somehow solve everything.

I opened my eyes and swayed up, drawing in a lungful of the beautiful air. The sight of my Grandmother tied to a horse only a few feet behind him...Her eyes snapped to mine, a green that flickered from an emerald so deep it was nearly black, to the gray-green of desert sage.

Uncle's grating chuckle scraped across me, a warning to every instinct I possessed.

I had breathed in, but when I let the air out, I did not breathe again. Dizziness bit into my brain, and I plopped back against the ground. *I wanted more air. Desperately.*

Spark had wanted to cavort in the fire with the dragonsbane forever. If I didn't want to dance to the tune my uncle set the rest of my life, I had to resist the false lure of the smoke.

Instead of rising to my feet, I turned my face to the dirt, hunting cleaner air. Grandmother may still smell of the forest, but given her current predicament she probably reeked more of the dust and sweat of the horse she rode. That smoke was not her.

My brain won the argument against my emotions, although barely. I stayed down, breathing shallowly, pretending to be overcome until Uncle stopped shoving the incense burner at me. Luckily he was too lazy to lean over, or my dryad would be even further away. Then again, he'd always kept his distance from us, never wanting to soil his person with our special brand of contamination.

He remounted his horse, safely away from me once again. "Drissa," he chided. "Drissa, child. You can't survive out here on your own." He jerked his head at the man standing guard over me. "Stay ready in case she tries to run."

The man who had stepped on me had already proven his worth to my uncle with his sharp eyes. He happily pulled a loop of leather free of his belt. He grinned down at me as I dared to turn and face my enemies.

He stretched the leather and snapped it. His broken nose was not one I recognized, which surprised me. How had he realized the innocent looking tree trunk falling over was me? Most men would have ignored it, even forewarned by my uncle.

Flicking his hand at another nearby lout, Uncle commanded, "Brandon, search her for weapons. Secure her packs where she can't reach them."

Brandon dismounted smoothly. He was older than most men Uncle Ralph hired; his beard was gray and pushing white. His teeth were still intact, and he sported a helmet with a thick horn sprouting out either side. His dark eyes were not hardened or shifty when he studied me. There was only caution.

Uncle sighed heavily. "Stand up, Drissa. Or I'll haul you up by your ankles."

Reluctantly standing, I knew what was coming. I ignored Brandon even as he headed right for me and instead twisted and ducked with my fists and arms over my head.

Brandon hesitated, but my raised hands were not wasted. The lash from Uncle crashed down, smacking my arm rather than my head. Even if there had been enough dryad in me to slide into bark and protect my arms, I didn't dare. Uncle needed to believe my dryad was dead and gone or he'd force more smoke on me.

I glared at him around my arms. "No, dear Uncle, I have not forgotten how to survive."

Brandon froze, his eyes passing from me to Uncle Ralph.

Knowing the real danger, I remained focused on my uncle. For a moment, I thought he might run me down with his horse, but the horse didn't like the lash, not even directed at me. The stallion danced sideways and snorted, forcing my uncle to concentrate on his seat.

He cursed roundly. "She keeps a dagger in her boot. Make sure you find it."

Brandon caught my eyes. His mouth twisted as though he were quite angry. His mood wasn't unusual. Most men working for Uncle were either drunk, desperate, perpetually angry or all of those things.

I scooted my leg a bit away from my body so he could grab the dagger. The exploding crystal from Zoe was tucked in the pocket of my trousers, under my tunic. The hard stone would be easily detected if this Brandon gave me a pat down. I should have secured the piece with the leather necklace that held Falk's feather. At least then it would appear to be harmless jewelry.

My heart skipped a beat when I thought of Falk. *Falk!*

The trees around me no doubt heard the cry, but I had, indeed, breathed too much smoke. Their reply was nothing more than leaves shifting in the wind.

The man knew his job. Brandon patted every part of me, a humiliation worse than being run over by a horse. His hand hesitated over the crystal, but he moved past it and then back again as he decided whether to let me keep it.

He could not know its use, but even a rock could be used as a weapon by the right hand. If he saw it was a crystal, he'd know it was more than just a stone.

"She's clean." He stepped away.

Uncle spat. "She's never been that. Nothing more than a useless weed, but if the prince takes her, that leaves Ava for later. Once I have my title, she'll bring an even greater price than this one. Tie the chit with her grandmother. To Glasdon!"

I stepped towards Grandmother on my own, but Brandon was not lacking in experience or intelligence. He accepted the leather from his compatriot and bound my hands before lifting me onto the horse behind Grandmother. Out of habit or training, he reached to check Grandmother's ropes.

I coughed and started to squirm.

His hand hovered for half a moment and then dropped back down. He did not glance back my way.

Not exactly an ally, but...he had not been as thorough as he could have been. He had not taken the time to test the bonds around Grandmother's hands. Nor had he inspected the rope looping under the horse's belly that had tied Grandmother's feet. Good thing because that rope was very nearly shredded from my earlier efforts.

Perhaps the brightest spot was that Uncle yelled, "Glasdon" again.

I had been headed there anyway. He was saving me the walk.

Chapter 23

Falk could hear before he could see. Breathable air and the strident harpy-like screeches of his aunt revived him. It was possible his aunt's voice had raised him from the dead, because he usually went to great lengths to avoid her. His own mother was melodramatic enough without throwing her sister into the mess, especially when either was on a rant.

Tinny static rang in his ears. His aching ribs reminded him that he had been squeezed in a death grip by a gryphon. The lack of oxygen rather than his aunt's nagging voice might be causing the ringing in his ears, but it all depended upon how long she had been raving.

"You cannot *kidnap* him into marriage! Oh, by the council and all its rules, how did my sister get involved with a gryphon!" Pans banged.

Was it too much to hope that she might smack Briella with a hot skillet? Falk's guts burned with angry fire. He pushed his fingers across the floor, hoping to find a weapon, but all he succeeded in doing was grinding his broken ribs.

Briella tried to get in a word edgewise, but Aunt May, true to form, kept right on talking around her protests.

"But what else was I to do?" Briella whined. "He was headed to a church! With that silly human girl! What if he lost his head?"

"Of course he's lost his head," Aunt May agreed in a shout loud enough to be heard in Glasdon. "Were it not for the steady guiding wings of my sister, where would he be now? I could have told my sister you girls are nothing but trouble!" There was a slapping sound that was probably a rolling pin against innocent dough. If Falk had his way, he'd take the pin to Briella's wings and make sure she thought twice before diving after a man. Had she planned to kill him? Or just keep him hidden until Drissa was safely married to a prince she didn't want?

Surely, Briella didn't think she'd live long enough to see that day because in one form or another he would kill her before he allowed Drissa to be forced into marriage to another man.

"No harm was done," Briella tried. "I brought him home."

Pleading. Good. That meant Aunt May was seriously bent on revenge. He didn't have time for justice right now, although he'd dearly love to teach Briella a lesson she wouldn't forget.

Drissa was one of the most competent women he had ever met, but he had no intention of leaving her to extricate herself from the clutches of her uncle. She had done that once; her preference in the matter had been decided.

"That man has been out of this house for an age and a day and has the right to choose a mate," his aunt raged. "Only a fool and an idiot would think otherwise."

Falk peeled back one eyelid, wishing he could so easily shut his ears. His hawk should have been at the fore, but once again, he was in human form with no memory of it happening. When he sat up, his ribs bellowed a protest. At least one was cracked, possibly more.

The shuttered room was his only excuse for failing to immediately notice his own mother perched on the edge of the large rocking chair that his father had carved and stuffed for her.

"It would appear I have made a grave error in judgment," she said quietly, handing him a cup. She didn't even try for a light tone. Her whisper was full of regret and worry.

The scent of rich licorice coffee revived him enough to ask, "What the hell happened?"

"Shh. We don't want her to know you've woken. It will be easier if you sneak out the back, and let me deal with this problem since it appears to be one of my own making." She offered him a plate of food. In any crisis, she baked. Hunted. Cooked. Preserved. And fed people.

Falk struggled to gain his feet. Dizziness assaulted him, but it numbed some of the painful scrapes and bruises. "The bitch has dragonsbane somewhere."

His mother lost her whisper to a hiss of anger. Her temper was legendary, and no doubt, she had been holding onto it by a thread. Hawk eyes flashed for an instant. "I'll add it to the list of sins."

"How did I get here?" Scalding hot agony from his ribs convinced him to keep his movements and breathing shallow. Changing would help the healing, but his hawk was completely dark. It was like a migraine, as if part of his vision, part of his brain, was missing completely. "Damn her hide." Drissa had better not have suffered a feather of damage or he'd hunt the gryphon bitch to an early grave.

His mother finally started talking. "A dragonkin came to the nest this morning, first light. We assumed there were problems with the rescue in Typhon. Shae—your father and I took off, following. The dragonkin led us instead to Briella. She was carrying you in a mad flight. The dragonkin began harassing her. We followed suit. Briella tried to claim she was rescuing you and had planned to deliver you here all along."

"Spark was here?"

She nodded and then shrugged. "It was the same dragonkin that was with you and the girl during the rescue of the other kin."

"Her name is Drissa." He choked back to keep from yelling. It was normally Hawk that wanted to scream a challenge, but he would shout Drissa's name from here to Glasdon if it would help find her faster.

His mother sniffed. "I was never properly introduced." She raised a hand before he had a chance to say something he might regret later. "That's no excuse, I know. I was in a snit." She glanced at the closed door leading to the kitchen. Aunt May was still going strong, banging pans and slamming things against the counters.

"Briella had me convinced that the girl—Drissa—had used the dragonsbane to put you under a spell. That's one of the reasons we insisted on accompanying you and the dragons to help rescue the kin. I was determined to save you from whatever dangers had befallen you!" His normally calm and in control mother was completely rattled.

"I did not require rescuing."

"I believed Briella! She's talked of nothing but you and the wedding these past few weeks. She gave every impression that the two of you were madly in love."

"I told you I had no plans to marry her."

"But when she set the date, and we began planning, you said nothing!"

"What more was there to say?"

"I thought you were staying away so that Briella could plan her surprises. That's what she told me."

He unclenched his teeth to answer. "I haven't stopped to visit in over six weeks whether she was underfoot or not."

His mother inspected her linked fingers, holding them together tightly as though they might fly apart on their own. Had they been in claw form, she would be clenching them against the arm of the chair and quite possibly snapping it to pieces. "Your brother tried to tell me the truth. Your father was starting to question the plans, and then this dragonsbane came along, and I simply panicked."

"Was I in this form when the dragonkin led you to the gryphon?"

She nodded. "How could she have used dragonsbane in flight? Or did she stop to burn the drug?"

He shrugged, causing flames of pain across his back and ribs. The skin and muscle were torn. "It doesn't have to be smoke. She had me in a death grip. I was desperate for air." He vaguely remembered a last chance to breathe as he attacked her foot. Even as things went black, she had let up for an second. There was no memory of sulfur, but a faint memory of a sharp chemical... "Ammonia? For a moment I smelled something odd, but for all I know, maybe she did land."

"Ammonia?" His mother's head jerked up. "The night after we finished the battle for the dragonkin she asked for smelling salts. She said it was in case they had to revive and move a dragonkin quickly from Typhon. I thought it was a good idea." She closed her eyes. "Fooled again."

"She could have mixed the dragonsbane in with the salts. Then when she needed it, she may have been able to shove the salts and dragonsbane at me without landing." His brain was so addled at the moment, plain smelling salts might be of use. "I need to go."

"How will you travel anywhere if you can't fly?"

"Same way I managed it the first time." He grabbed one of his father's daggers, along with a bow and arrow from the weapons cabinet. "It would be a good idea if Briella is gone when I get back." He started to gesture with his head, but a sharp twinge reminded him that most movement was a bad idea.

"Council is voting to make use of dragonsbane punishable by death," his mother said.

"You'll take this to them?" He stopped in surprise. Hawks usually handled matters on their own.

She smiled her crafty smile, looking more like his mother than she had since he'd woken. "No. But she will be gone when you return."

"What keeps her in there?" He'd never stay and listen to his own aunt rant unless he was bound and tied and possibly unconscious. Curiosity sparked briefly, but even knowing how resourceful his mother was, he couldn't imagine how they had restrained her. Even in human form, Briella could call on the strength of her gryphon, and there were few creatures who could argue against a gryphon's notorious strength.

"Her choice has been taken from her as it was from you. Only we didn't know about the dragonsbane or we might have used that too."

Triumph that the enemy would suffer raged through him. Hawk itched to be released. He ignored the pain in his back, and using one of the new sheaths from the cabinet, strapped the dagger and arrows across his shoulder. The sheath was one from Zoe and would stay in place even when he could finally shift to hawk. He needed to fly, but the chemical was like a veil. He could breathe through it, but not fully use the air. His hawk was as necessary as breathing.

He'd walk then, until he could fly. If Drissa could survive in this form and succeed as she had, then he could do no less.

"I do believe I should say goodbye." He strode to the kitchen door and slammed it open before his mother had a chance to protest, not that he would have listened.

At the disruption, his Aunt May lifted her chin, but then snapped her mouth closed. Her curly brown locks had no doubt started the day pulled back, but with her anger, they had fluffed like feathers all around her head.

Falk eyed the crystals that locked bright beams around Briella. "Zoe?" he asked his mother without turning around.

"The dragonkin flew for Zoe as soon he was certain we understood the problem. Zoe was happy to help, and Briella was so busy playing innocent, we had her trapped before she could escape."

Briella was tied to a chair in addition to the spell that held her captive. Instead of the usual half-lidded seductive gaze he often received from her, he witnessed a wide-eyed try for innocence. Her lips parted, and she heaved her large bosom as she took a deep breath, ready to plead her case.

He cut her off. "You are dead to me."

She gasped and recoiled from his anger.

"Even your shadow is dead to me. Should it fall on my territory ever again, you will lose it."

He did not wait for her reply, but stalked back through the door.

Briella shifted, her warrior eagle cry echoing through the tree.

He was not afraid. That cage would keep her contained no matter how much anger and energy she wasted.

"If I had dragonsbane, I do believe I'd make her breathe it," he said, yanking open the door to the outside.

His mother cocked her head sideways. "She must have kept some when we were trying to destroy it. She may still have some."

"She is dead to me," Falk repeated.

His mother nodded and closed the kitchen door. His aunt, for once, remained silent.

Chapter 24

Just before stepping outside, Falk asked, "Any chance Spark stayed around? He can reach Drissa faster than I can." He despised asking for help, but Drissa was in grave danger. Now was not the time for pride.

Miserably, his mother shook her head. "The kin left the moment the gryphon was secured."

"He will have gone in search of Drissa, then."

"Your father is on watch outside. Take him with you." Her hands feathered as she allowed stress to rule the moment. The tears swimming in her eyes indicated her anger had reached a dangerous level. "Falk—forgive me."

Falk didn't take time to reassure her. His jaw clenched. Nothing would happen to Drissa. She had escaped her vile uncle once; she had it in her to do it again. She kept secrets, but she had sense enough to put her trust in him, and he would not let her down. He already knew who to blame for this mess, and her uncle would pay the price in full.

He strode outside where his father waited, more than half hawk, balanced in a tree, ready to take off. "I cannot leave your mother alone."

"I know. Is it likely any gryphons will come to Briella's rescue?"

"Not taking any chances. Your mother can handle the one easily, but if more show up, we'll evacuate and strike later."

"Count me in if that happens."

"Go then. Fly safe."

He shook his head. "She used dragonsbane. I'll be on foot for a while."

His father's squawk of outrage echoed inside Falk's heartbeat. Ah, that was a good sign. His hawk was more awake than before. Falk flexed his fingers, but his wings were yet ghosts. He set a painfully fast jog, feeling more than seeing his father take to the skies.

Before he had covered even a half mile, Midnight the dragonkin landed. Clutched in his wing claw was an oval, speckled dragon's egg. It was in better shape than Midnight. The dragonkin was covered in dust. His face, instead of healing, was scarred with patches of scabbing scales and newly broken skin.

"Did you have to dig it out?" Falk asked.

Midnight rumbled an answer, but Falk didn't know what to make of it. He took his best guess. "You've retrieved the egg, but cannot guard it?"

The kin stood straighter and showed his teeth.

"You do guard it." Falk launched into a quick explanation of what had happened to he and Drissa. "I go to find her. If you need my help, be plain. I have no time to waste."

Midnight carefully lowered the egg and nudged it to Falk with his snout.

"You wish me to keep it safe." Falk needed a dragonkin egg about as much as he needed to be struck by the curse of dragonsbane. "I need to get to Drissa." But he was already leaning over to collect the egg. His blood boiled with the delay, a panicked worry flooding through him. Even his hawk, a born fighter, could not reassure him. He needed to reach Drissa faster than his hawk could fly. For a moment, leaning over, his vision went dark. Maybe it was from his cracked ribs. Maybe it was from the blood rushing to his head too quickly. Or maybe it was a warning of how dark his life would be without her.

Drissa. He could afford no delay!! Of course, Drissa had probably felt that way even as she carried him to safety when it wasn't in her best interest to do so. She had also protected the kin.

He stared down at the egg and felt its warmth. He could not leave it unprotected. Gritting his teeth he asked Midnight, "Can you find Drissa? The dragonsbane keeps me landlocked."

Midnight hissed.

"Do not worry. I can protect it anyway." Falk couldn't deposit the egg at his parents' house, not with the gryphon situation. He was close enough to the redwood. It would not cost him much time to drop it there. Perhaps in the meanwhile, he would clear his system and his hawk would return.

It hurt to breathe, but Falk ran anyway. His vision tunneled, but he could not fail Midnight anymore than he could fail Drissa. He was nearly at his front door when he realized Midnight was not following or flying overhead.

Where had the dragonkin gone?

Drissa's missing essence when he reached the redwood spiked through him like a knife. She could have explained to the tree exactly what was needed. He could explain until the sun went down and would only be granted bare hints that Redwood understood.

"Dragonkin egg," he told the tree. "Needs to be kept warm and safe. No one can take it." Falk added several large rocks to the stove and placed the egg gently inside the circle. The stones would retain heat. He then lit the stove, throwing wood bits inside until the flames happily roared.

"Protect the egg," he instructed.

As he left, the tree shut the door, almost ushering him out. Falk looked back to find that the lines of the door had faded. His home, Redwood the tree, had just sealed the door. Well, they had an understanding then.

Automatically, out of habit, Falk reached for Hawk. Half of him changed before blackness slammed into him and stole his breath. He would have fallen had Redwood not been a wall upon which to lean.

Panting, he allowed his human side control. If he tried to shift again, it might kill him. "Damn you, Briella."

Before the blackness completely receded, Spark landed, followed by Lindis.

Though he was still gasping for air, he was glad to see them both.

Spark gave a worried dragon-hiss and pushed against Falk's leg.

"We will find Drissa." He wasn't certain if he was reassuring himself or the dragonkin.

Lindis spoke without changing. "You are not healing yourself."

"Dragonsbane," he gasped out.

"Dragonsbane? The gryphon used dragonsbane?"

Falk nodded through the puff of her sulfur smoke, coughing politely to remind her that he didn't wish to breathe fire and brimstone.

"You will fly with me then. Any idea how long to change?"

He stumbled forward. "Hawk is close, but not close enough." He didn't waste time on wishful thinking. Lindis was here, and she was the fastest route to Drissa.

Giving him a scant heartbeat to settle, she took off.

Spark followed in her wake, squawking worriedly.

"How did you find me?" Falk asked.

"This time or when you were in the clutches of the gryphon?"

"Either."

"Spark found you sometime late last night, near morning. He had been nagging me to check on you and Drissa since yesterday when Briella didn't show up for duty. Last night, after we were finished in Typhon, Spark started hunting. When he found you in the clutches of the gryphon, he alerted your parents and Zoe because they were closer, and then came for me."

"After working with you all day rescuing dragonkin, he flew all night looking for us?"

Lindis sighed, but it was more of an impatient hiss. "It was my oversight. I should have listened to him. Spark didn't like the fact that Briella was with your mother the other morning when your mother brought breakfast."

"She was not."

"To you, no. But as far as Spark was concerned, he smelled them both. He took a disliking to Briella after the battle at the auction site, and he didn't like her close to your lair. When she didn't show up to help us as promised, he was convinced Briella must be hunting you. But I was tired after a day of negotiating for the dragonkin."

"You gave the chimera options?"

"Of course. Send out the dragonkin or fight to the death. We agreed to leniency if they turned in any other kin location and allowed us to search all premises for dragonsbane."

"So how many did you kill?"

She shrugged. "It was the first day. They all opted to send out the dragonkin with instructions to kill us. Simple enough for us to give the kin new instructions, and easy for us to avoid the smoke of their dragonsbane. None of the chimera were prepared. In their arrogance they assumed the kin would suffer any damage while they had time to escape."

"Surely the chimera have figured out by now that the last instruction the dragonkin hears is the one it will obey."

"Not my problem. I suspect they believe they are keeping the kin well in hand, and what servants would dare change the instructions? They use the dragonkin as slaves and showpieces. No one until now has been likely to yell 'free yourself.' The chimera are cowards. When they chose to use the kin as the front battle line, we moved the line."

Falk could not fault her logic. What he knew of the chimera was too petty to be believed. "I bet they spend half their time stealing the dragonkin from their neighbors."

Lindis banked sharply before answering. "The kin were kept locked up, usually in dungeon conditions or fancy display cages. The chimera are accustomed to infighting so the rich guard their hovels well."

As Lindis straightened Falk felt his hawk automatically responding to the drafts. It was time. "I'm going hawk."

"As you wish."

Lindis was faster than he in any form, but he preferred being on his own.

"Spark found you before he could find Drissa," she said. "You can lead the way to where you last saw her."

Falk realized Lindis didn't know about Drissa's uncle. He explained quickly. "If her uncle captured her, she's no longer on foot. They'll be moving much faster mounted on horses. My best guess is that Briella decided to cut a deal with Drissa's uncle instead of helping you free the kin. She had a full day to locate him. Our route to Glasdon would not be difficult to guess. She snatched me right out of the sky at first light, leaving Drissa to her uncle."

Lindis hissed. "The gryphon was present when we discussed the contents of the log book. She overheard enough to know his name and the whereabouts of the church."

"And she stole the dragonsbane while the rest of us worked to destroy it."

"Is there any chance Drissa could have avoided her uncle by shifting to her tree form?"

"Such a maneuver would not fool him. He knows she is dryad. I doubt he followed Briella without a solid plan."

"You believe she is captured then?"

Falk screeched a war cry as he finished shifting. "Not for long."

Lindis breathed fire. "I have a score to settle with that prince. He has caused me quite enough trouble."

Falk settled into his form, letting the wind soothe and carry him closer with each beat of his wings.

Chapter 25

At least when Grandmother and I were in close proximity, we could communicate in dryad. I told her about the dragonkin and everything we knew about the dragonsbane. Of course, there was no leaving out Lindis, Zoe, Derrick, the ogres and Falk. His name was bound to come up sooner or later, especially once it was obvious that Grandmother knew about the gryphon.

"The gryphon must be the woman who found your uncle at the church yesterday. He'd been busy trading for anything from Wendal that he could get his hands on for the last two days, but he dragged us all up there in preparation of the ceremony tomorrow. The woman showed up, all flash and boobs, promising to sell him your location."

"I hope he didn't pay much," I muttered. "Falk was helping me travel to Glasdon once we found out that Uncle Ralph had a trade planned there for dragonsbane. Uncle was using my name for the trade!"

"He already traded for the dragonsbane," Grandmother informed me. "He's been trading in that a while; I'd guess before he even promised you to Prince Irwin."

"Are you certain?"

"Positive. He even planted some wolfsbane himself. I thought he was planning on poisoning me because I didn't realize he was using dried dragonkin blood to feed it. When he ran out of the kin's blood, he decided to use my blood to feed the plant."

"That's why it smells like you!"

"And it's the reason it keeps me from my dryad. But the longer he grew it without refreshing it with the dragonkin blood, the less potent the magic. When his last shipment didn't show up, he was forced to come back to Wendal to trade for more. The magic seems to come from the dragonkin's blood combined with mine."

I was surprised Uncle had been clever enough to use Grandmother's blood. "When dragonsbane is burned, all the shifters are forced to their human side. It didn't bother me until Uncle wafted his version of the smoke at me."

"We are not shifters like the weres and the others. We are even further from dragons in some ways, but closer in others."

"Close enough that even a lazy man with not a speck of magic decided to experiment."

"Do not imagine the idea was entirely his own, Drissa. The king may not have kidnapped his own son to marry a dragon, but that doesn't mean he wouldn't like to be able to control something so large and dangerous as shifters. Others have been experimenting with the dragonsbane for a while in an attempt to please the king. Your Uncle Ralph has been in cahoots with more than one such mage. He has tried to control me since he met me. Dragonsbane just so happened to go hand in hand with his goals."

"I'd rather align with the dragons than Uncle Ralph," I muttered.

"Agreed. In any case, he's been sniffing out disreputable mages all across Anton. One of them, and I think I know who, suggested he try my blood for growing the dragonsbane. I'm equally certain your uncle sold some of my blood in exchange for some of the dried dragonkin blood when he ran out the last time."

"You've been under his control since I left, haven't you?" The midday heat wasn't terribly hot, but sorrow and fear began to sweat from my every pore.

"If you hadn't left when you did, you'd have been captured alongside me, and we'd both be the worse for it."

I shivered, but had a hard time imagining a situation more dire than the one we found ourselves in now. "Dragonsbane forces shifters to their human side, just as it forced you, but thankfully it does not control their minds. Only the dragonkin seemed compelled to answer the call of the dragonsbane and take orders, perhaps because it is their blood that was used."

Her anger bled across our link, hot enough to spark a fire. "By all the roots that bind, I cannot imagine being forced to obey even a single one of his evil orders. The dragonsbane imbued with my blood already leaves me too much at his mercy and causes beastly headaches besides."

"How long does it last?"

Her answer felt for a moment as if the question was too difficult, much like when I asked one of the forest trees for something outside their experience. "He continues to force the stuff on me."

Left unsaid was that now I had been captured, he had no reason to keep her captive—or alive.

Before I came to Wendal, her fleeting thoughts and feelings would have been beyond my dryad senses. My dryad had been a foreign form to me, like dressing up on the outside with the real me still inside. I'd been dryad often of late and reaching out to the forest had taught me a lot.

Reading her flash of worry was easier now. Her feelings of doom washed over my skin like a wind carrying the scent of death. Uncle had only tolerated her in the past because someone had to see to our education and care. With my sister and me older now, the landscape was changing. Once I was safely married off to Prince Irwin, Uncle had no use for Grandmother, especially if he planned to rid himself of Ava in another such marriage of convenience.

"We won't let it come to that," I said softly. My hands were bound, but I leaned into her back and sent my own reassurances, a flood of love and all my determination.

Her answer was one of strength, the dryad I knew so well.

A few short moments later, one of her hands snaked back quickly. She waited for me to grasp the knife handle. She had finally managed to free herself, and it was now my turn.

Chapter 26

The ride to Glasdon should have allowed plenty of time to worry about Falk and Ava, but Grandmother was not one to sit around and wait for Uncle to make things worse. Her dryad powers were weak at best, but with us able to communicate, she felt we had enough resources between the two of us to take action.

"We're running out of time and forest. The closer we get to Glasdon, the harder it will be to escape."

She was right, but what could we do? My dryad was coming back as my head cleared, but the thought of Uncle Ralph realizing it and using the dragonsbane again caused panic in my chest. "Should we break away and run?" Our hands were no longer tied, and we could slash the lead rope tying us to Uncle's mount.

"They will only chase us. We need them running from us. What have you learned while you have been traveling? Can you bend the trees to your will? Your communication is much better. Your dryad is stronger now."

I sighed. "I cannot even walk when I am tree. The forest listens to me, and sometimes the trees help, but it's their own goodwill, not me."

Grandmother smiled in my head. "That is always the best way, and the reason I never pushed you to learn more. But you are dryad."

"Only a quarter."

"Some things you are born with, but the rest is learned. You have the talent. It's time to own it. We need to bend the trees and knock the men from the horses. We can imbue the trees with the power to fight as we cannot."

Redwood certainly seemed to manage more than a few simple feats, but he was special, perhaps even a dryad of a different sort. "I can ask the trees, but there's something missing. I don't know how to help them help us. When we rescued the dragonkin, the trees asked me for something I didn't know how to give." I still had no idea how to provide what they needed.

"It is doable. Try," she instructed. The words were ones she had drilled into me in the past.

My dryad side knew well how to reach for the boughs and limbs around me, but it was harder now because instead of the warm soil beneath my feet, there was a creaking leather saddle and a horse. Everything good, green and growing was so far away from me. *"Bend and sway,"* I suggested, pushing myself. My hands began to knot into wood even though changing hadn't been my intent at all.

Grandmother didn't chide me. Instead, I felt her dryad presence much stronger than my own. "Borrow it," she whispered. "Take me to the trees."

Not even sure I could reach the wood and greenery myself, I closed my eyes and pictured them swaying. I envisioned the branches reaching out and smacking Uncle. A stray branch only needed to grow the slightest bit to snag the clothing, push the men and make the horses nervous.

"Use the energy you normally use to turn tree," Grandmother encouraged. "But this time, you grow them instead of you."

Ah, that made sense to me! I could smell the woodsy freshness of Grandmother, but this time her essence was stronger and without the taint of "other" that was in the smoke Uncle had used. There was her soft hug, her crooked smile and her laughing eyes, but at the same time she was heartwood, strong and thick with an energy that surged through me.

I sent it to the forest around us, letting it flow from my fingertips out to passing branches.

Like a shot of sunlight or nutrients from the soil, the trees sang with it, growing, snaking out and finally, my timing was right. One of the flanking riders took a tree branch right in the face.

My success was energy. I continued to push it outward, and for the first time, I felt what it was like to convert sunlight into...power. Just as thin branches began slapping a man on our right, Uncle screamed with rage.

"Filthy wench!" He spun his horse around.

We had concentrated too long as dryads. My human eyes were closed, and my essence had become moving heartwood, a rich part of the world around me that I had never before experienced.

Grandmother's focus was suddenly snatched away, leaving me dizzy.

I blinked in confusion. The sun that had been a source of power was now hot against my skin. Some part of me continued to draw on it, but without proper concentration, I failed to convert it to a power my human side could use.

Grandmother snarled, throwing an arm out that was solid wood. I gathered my wits and changed my own arms.

Uncle freed his battle ax. The only thing slowing him was the dancing of hooves beneath him as the horse tried to obey commands. We were still tied to his horse, making riding back towards us difficult.

Both of us knew all too well that he would butcher the horse that carried us without remorse. I dove off, clutching Grandmother. Even angry, Uncle Ralph might remember I had a purpose and withhold a killing strike. If he pulled back, perhaps I could save us both.

We hit the ground hard. I couldn't hear Grandmother anymore, even though we were touching. "Grandmother!"

There was nothing but a dizzy blackness where she had been.

I barely remembered to roll, but my desperate maneuvers weren't enough to escape from the danger of a slashing ax and pounding hooves. Uncle raged by, hooves barely missing us, dirt choking me.

But the soil was my friend. I knew how to grow around Grandmother and protect her. I had done it for Falk.

But...her source of guidance was gone. I fumbled, feeling for the power she had lent me, the flow to communicate with the other trees. Though branches around us still swayed as though part of a storm, they no longer grew.

Uncle's horse reared as he reined it back, yanking hard to turn back for another pass. Rocks and dust churned.

There was no time! There were so many things I hadn't had time to learn, too many questions left to ask.

I hardened my bark even though it was too late. Frantic, I reached for my dagger. It was a paltry and useless weapon against the horse and rider bearing down on me.

My searching fingers wrapped around Zoe's crystal.

I did not wish to injure the horse. Its eyes were wide with fear, the bit in its mouth reminding me of Spark and the other innocent dragonkin. How much power did the crystal hold? Could I throw it at Uncle Ralph without injuring anyone else?

A limb. A staff at just the right height and length might work. I grew an appropriate branch even as the thought occurred to me.

The ax swung back.

Zoe said to feel the word, mean the word, make it a part of me. I was dryad. I rooted myself deep in case the explosion blew me backwards. Thinking of the focus Grandmother had lent me, I whispered the word with all my strength.

Chapter 27

Grandmother hadn't told me that the power of dryad didn't have to come from sunshine and soil. When the crystal exploded in a rainbow of colors, the white of something akin to sunlight blasted across me, powering my arm first and traveling through the rest of me faster than photosynthesis ever dreamed of moving. The crystal itself was soil in one form and instead of exploding out and away, somehow I absorbed it as though I were one giant root.

My arm grew twenty years in less than a second, shoving its way right through my uncle's face, knocking him off his mount and nearly taking off his head. His little helmet may have been spelled to make a tree bounce harmlessly off his head, but it did nothing against the battering ram branch that tried to grow right through him.

The resounding crack when he hit the ground left him unmoving. The battle ax spun through the air, missing me by a hair.

My roots stretched. The rest of me stretched. The ground beneath my feet shredded as roots barreled through it, over it, under it. Horses screamed. Brandon's opened-mouthed shock raced by my senses. He yelped as a root burst through the ground between his feet.

The grizzled man had been kind to me even though he was partly responsible for my current predicament. I forced the root back into the soil before it grew large enough to permanently unman him.

The tiny voice of my grandmother screamed at me from somewhere below. "Reel yourself in! Don't contain that! Give it to the trees!"

"What?! How???" Desperately, I lashed out, pushing the power along my fingertips as I had done before, hoping to release it into the nearby growth.

The living mass of forest was greedy, sucking it up like liquid sunlight, but without Grandmother guiding me, it was not the smooth transition of before. The power kept expanding outward. I'd give a little away, but my trunk and arms still burst through the forest canopy with uncontrollable growth. Below me, the trees waved back and forth in the throes of a storm, branches snapping, adding greenery and creating a wind that blew everything away from me, the center.

"Slow down!" Grandmother snapped the command in that voice that had always made me freeze in my guilty tracks.

All it did this time was cause me to pull in some of the power I'd been trying to give away. Leaves burst forth and expanded to the size of dinner plates. Holding them up wasn't a problem, but avoiding smacking the large dragon square in the face was impossible.

Wait! Dragon? "Lindis?!?"

She tucked in hard, tried to break her forward momentum with her wings and ended up in a tumbling backwards dive with no time to answer.

A happy peep was Spark, who dove right into the swirling air, somersaulted once and almost managed to snag a branch as he shot by. He corrected quickly and took the next one down, somewhere in the depths of my many branches.

"*Drissa?*" Falk's squawk was more shock than happiness. He hit the vortex of churning air displaced by my rapid growth and flipped feet over beak. He smacked into me, and I narrowly avoided suffocating him with a sprouting of thick leaves.

"Graaaandmaaaa, heeelp!" Reaching out to her like a submerged tree limb, I hunted to find the special dryad link from before.

My desperation hit her hard, but she was a grandmother. She had dealt with childbirth, the death of her own daughter, and the needs of two growing granddaughters. She was back on her feet, if barely, and had enough love to encompass a lot of power. Her dryad was wrapped in mine, and she began taming the excess power, sucking it in and directing it out in a much more orderly manner than I could manage.

The woods around us had already expanded, the trees taller by several feet. Grandmother's power swept along one of my roots and directed the power further away.

"Reel yourself in, child."

I tried to answer, but my dryad was busy. My branches waved, keeping the windstorm going, rocking everything within reach.

"*Focus, Drissa.* There is work yet to be done!"

I sucked in a deep breath of calming air, not realizing that at my size it caused quite an oxygen displacement. "Reel in. Right. Focus."

From somewhere down below a dragon bellowed, followed by a human curse. "What in hell is that thing?"

Falk found his footing. Spark danced from branch to branch. I tried to shrink myself back into myself. Grandmother kept spinning the magic.

My stomach knotted so hard I needed to throw up. The power was too much, too fast. My trunk swayed dangerously.

Falk worried across a branch, "Easy, Drissa." His claws held on tight as the air blew several feathers right off.

Grandmother paused, waiting for me to catch up. Her every breath echoed in my dryad.

"Reach out to the forest," she whispered in my head. "Find the heart of it and shelter in its beat. There is more power to be found there than even this."

I thought of Falk's home and how huge Redwood was, how he moved the earth without a tremble, how he existed within the forest, but was a part of it and the earth. I felt the warm sunshine and breathed in the scents of clean air, earth, wood and water. She was right. There was much, much more. Even as huge as I had grown, I was a small part of an important whole.

Slowly, in bits and pieces, I let the power leak near and then farther. Like reversing time, my trunk and branches shrank.

By the time my dryad had leveled to normal size, Falk had gone human and so had Lindis.

She waited suspiciously nearby, holding, of all things, Uncle's battle ax.

Chapter 28

I collapsed into Falk's waiting arms. The world spun sideways, upside down and finally, right side up. Spark planted himself firmly behind my legs, puffing a hello and pushing me into Falk, not that I needed any encouragement.

"Are you okay?" Falk's murmur in my ear sent tremors down my legs. I wasn't sure if this was because the earth was still moving or because he moved me in ways that the earth didn't. I clung to him, ever so happy to see him.

Grandmother groaned from behind and below me. Letting him support me still, I struggled to turn, finding Spark's big eyes nearly as high as my own. His silver-gray scales were dusty and though he had grown, his girth was a bit on the scrawny side compared to the times when he had just finished stuffing himself.

I brushed my hand across his dear head, peering around his bulk to find my grandmother. "Grandmother?"

"What. Was that?" She sat on the ground, her legs straight out, one hand pressed against the side of her head. For the first time, I noticed she wore her favorite gardening pants, the brown leathers that were so streaked with time, they resembled bark. Her green tunic was torn and lopsided. Red streaks still marred her wrists where ropes had been bound too tight. Technically, she still hadn't gone full dryad, so she hadn't been able to heal.

"Zoe gave me a crystal in case of a fight," I explained.

"A lantern?" She squinted in confusion and pressed her other palm to the opposite side of her head as though trying to make sure it stayed in one piece on her shoulders.

"No, Zoe is a mage. It was an energy crystal designed to explode if I needed to protect myself or stall attackers. I was trying to throw it at Uncle Ralph, hoping it would blast him, but I had to say the word of power and when I did, the thing exploded backwards. Or something."

Grandmother made an odd noise, and finally trusting my balance, I extracted myself from Falk's arms and knelt beside her.

She stared at me with eyes as green as new leaves and laughed. Half of the chuckle was choked back as if her mirth somehow hurt her, but she couldn't stop completely. "You drew the power in instead of pushing it out."

"I wasn't supposed to have to do anything but throw the crystal and say the word!"

"Yes, well, your mage friend didn't take into account that when you're dryad and in the middle of your own magic, you need magic. Your dryad sucked up every bit of that explosion."

"And you grew into that monstrous tree?" Lindis folded her arms, the ax resting against her leg. "Interesting. What happened to your uncle?"

I blinked. Grandmother stopped chuckling, and we both searched the area. He had been coming at us with the ax, but he was gone now. "Well," I wrinkled my forehead, concentrating. "I did hit him with the crystal, but it was tucked inside a fast-growing branch at the time. He went backwards off his horse, and then I lost track of him. His men scattered, even Brandon."

"Brandon?" Falk asked.

"Uncle Ralph demanded Brandon search me for weapons. He found the crystal, but didn't say anything. Although he did take my spare dagger. When I went tree..." My brow furrowed again. "It's hard to say, but I probably avoided hurting him. I grew so fast, there was no way to keep track of everything."

Grandmother raised one hand in my direction. I reached to help her stand. Spark, being Spark, got behind her and pushed, which was not as helpful as he seemed to think, but it did give her something to lean against once she was on her feet.

"I don't believe I've been introduced to your friends," she said, dusting her hands against her trousers.

Spark was first, given that he was nudging her backside in his version of propping her up. "Spark the dragonkin, Lindis and Falk." Since I wouldn't dream of introducing myself or Grandmother as dryad, I applied the same logic and left off any mention of shifting ability. "Everyone, meet Burgundy Featherkile, my grandmother."

My grandmother was nothing if not classy. She nodded regally at each of them, saving a slightly suspicious glance for Falk.

I had been so relieved to see him, I hadn't bothered to hide my enthusiasm. Or my affection. "How did you escape Briella's clutches?" I demanded.

Falk scowled. "It's a long story. I've Spark to thank for my rescue. In short, he called in the troops and after a battle that was more social posturing than bloody, she was captured."

"More's the pity," I muttered over the lack of blood. I smiled at Spark. He was uttering nonsense noises, no doubt his version of the story, from behind Grandmother.

Grandmother gave him a pat and then paced a step or two away. When she touched the nearest oak, she was not satisfied with whatever information she received. "We must get to the church in Glasdon. If your uncle somehow manages to arrive first, he'll either force the marriage or kidnap Ava to a place we might never find her."

"I'm beginning to feel like a burro," Lindis complained. "And carrying two of you is pushing my limits."

"Hello," a voice called out. It was followed by the movement of someone pushing through the underbrush. A few moments later Brandon emerged from behind a thicket of raspberries that had grown so tall, they had tumbled over and started again. "Would horses help?"

The forest around us was completely overgrown due to my feeding it, and I had been too focused on my friends to be wary. Still, to miss hearing a man leading three mounts nearby was inexcusable.

Falk was...I turned to find him gone, apparently not as unaware as me, or at least faster on the uptake. A swift glance at Lindis' face led me to believe she wasn't caught entirely off-guard, either.

I searched the trees for Falk, but couldn't spot him. He had to be somewhere near Brandon, ready to do battle if necessary.

Grandmother was even more angry about failing to hear the newcomer than me. Her face was full of thunder, and she swore out loud. "Drissa, if you failed to accidentally kill your uncle, I'm going to see the end of him." Her fists clenched, and bark crept across her arms before settling back.

"Can you not yet fully change? I whispered out loud and in silent dryad.

She didn't bother to whisper. "I probably can. But the trees have yet to recognize me as part of the forest. I just asked them about your uncle's whereabouts, and they failed to mention a man with three horses." Her eyes were wide and distraught. "I don't usually have to ask about what is wandering nearby. The heart of the forest conveys its secrets without me even thinking about it."

Brandon kept his hands in the open, but his sword remained at his hip. The horses nipped at nearby grasses that swayed well above their knees while we all watched one another other warily.

"This would be Brandon," I said by way of breaking the silence. "Generally speaking, he was the reason I was able to escape." Being wary of him now seemed a waste of time, but the man had been with my uncle.

Falk stepped out of the trees on my right. "He's alone."

"How did you manage to retrieve the horses?" I asked Brandon. Everything within a mile had taken to its heels when my dryad began to grow. Brandon hadn't seemed inclined to stick around himself.

"Once the horses felt safe, they settled down." He gave the lead horse a pat. "Ice Maiden has been with me a while. She befriended these other two, and while I'd like to believe she was patiently waiting for me, the grasses were green and nothing else was busy eating them. They took it upon themselves to do the job."

"And you saw no point in leaving them behind," Falk said. "But why return here?"

I interrupted before Brandon could answer. "You work for my uncle." My accusation branded him guilty of a heinous crime.

"Worked, as in past tense, job over." His jaw clenched and his dark eyes flicked with impatience. "It would seem your beloved Uncle Ralph was not, in fact, rescuing his nieces from a greedy grandmother who wished to sell them off. And I do believe I'm headed in the same direction you plan to go. Use the horses to Glasdon. If I can be of service, so be it. If it's all the same to you, I'd then like to keep these two extra mounts to make up for lost wages."

"You could have freed me long ago," Grandmother pointed out.

He nodded his horned helmet in her direction. "Had I but known the truth, I would have." He reached up to one of the horses and untied a pack. More specifically, *my* pack. He stepped forward three steps and set it down carefully, another obvious peace offering.

"We haven't time to argue about this," I grumbled. Watching him for sudden movement, I walked just close enough to retrieve my belongings. The dagger that was normally housed in my boot, the one he had taken from me, was strapped to the side.

I picked up my belongings and backed up without ever taking my eyes off him. "We need to get to Ava *now* before men more loyal to Uncle Ralph reach her. Even if Uncle is lying dead under a bush, some of the men will realize her value."

Brandon nodded. "He did not leave her unguarded, but he had kept her hidden with your grandmother until recently. My first clue that something was amiss was when Prince Irwin arrived bound hand and foot at the inn where we were staying in Glasdon. Your uncle took him and your sister up to the church yesterday. The whole operation began to look less like a rescue and more like the bill of sale he claimed he was trying to prevent."

"How many men did he leave behind guarding them?" Falk asked.

Grandmother answered. "At least Saul and Jake. They arrived night before last with Prince Irwin in tow."

"And those two frogs well know what is going on," I snapped in disgust. "They are always in charge of trouble."

"What will happen if they get word that we're on our way?" Lindis demanded.

"They'll either go through with the marriage or bolt or both," I replied. "It depends on where they believe the most money can be made."

"In that case they will want the prince married and controlled." She breathed a single flame. "Again."

I had found my dryad in a manner I had never expected. I had found friends, and I had even rescued Grandmother. But I could not fly, nor travel particularly quickly. Dare we take his offer and use the horses?

Lindis turned to Brandon. "I'm not certain you are trustworthy, but you did return bearing an offer. It will not be forgotten, but do not think you are entirely trusted."

Brandon nodded. "There were four other hired men watching the girl and the prince. Two of them are new; your uncle hired them from Glasdon. The priest must be one of his men too, because he was not from Glasdon."

Lindis rolled her eyes. "They never are. Bought men," she snarled.

Grandmother was suddenly at my side, her hand on my arm. In dryad she said, "Dragon coming, flying low."

I knew of no enemies that were dragon, "What color is it?" I asked her. Aloud I said, "Dragon coming."

My words were a waste of time. Midnight announced his own entry, and instead of a graceful landing, he clipped a tree branch, swooped close over Falk's head and then landed at a fast clipped run before coming to rest against a large bush, panting in total exhaustion.

One wing was tucked in, but the other remained out at an angle. A dragon's egg was nestled in each wing claw.

Chapter 29

Lindis groaned and smacked her forehead in disbelief. "Not more. Midnight, I explicitly told you to rest before hunting more eggs."

Midnight's scales were a dull black, shining even less than when we first rescued him. He looked as though a cave roof had collapsed on top of him, covering him with layer upon layer of dust.

I rushed over to retrieve one of the eggs before he dropped it. It wasn't terribly large, but it was heavy. I quickly handed it to Spark. His wing claws were big enough to handle the egg, but he struggled to hold it and inspect it at the same time. Eventually he set it down.

"Don't these need to be warm?" I worried, staring at the egg.

Spark must have agreed with my assessment because he happily fired away at it, warming my toes rather more than necessary.

With a yelp, I jumped aside and accepted the other egg from Midnight. I wiped some of the dust from his snout with my own dirty hand. His jaw was nowhere near healed where the harness had punctured it. "You need to eat," I whispered. "And sleep. And heal."

"Where is he getting all these dragonkin eggs?" Falk asked.

Lindis shook her head at Midnight. "He's been out hunting them." She plucked the egg from my hand.

"Will it be okay?" I asked.

Lindis inspected the pebbly shell. "As long as they aren't cracked, they can remain dormant for quite some time without heat."

Falk studied the egg near Spark. "Midnight showed up this morning with one and left it in my care. At least that is what I perceived was required."

"This morning? You didn't sleep last night either?" Lindis whirled to face the dragonkin again.

Midnight crouched in on himself, too tired to offer any kind of defense.

"And you've your own egg to care for," she reprimanded more gently.

"He found it?" I clapped my hands in delight. "That is wonderful news!"

"If he lives to take care of it," she growled. "After you asked if his egg might still be hidden, he went straight back to his lair and located it. So instead of helping us rescue more dragonkin yesterday, he made it his mission to check other lairs for possible eggs. Dragon eggs are very well concealed, and he's exhausting himself digging them out. I instructed him to bring them to me for protection, but I didn't expect to be roaming around half of Wendal."

She glared at me as though this was somehow my fault.

"I didn't steal any dragonkin," I protested.

"He cannot possibly care for them all, especially while looking for others." She stared down at the egg. "Have you any idea how much a dragonkin eats after it hatches?"

I looked at Spark. "Well, yes."

"And we dare not keep them all in one place either, especially now." Lindis put her hands on her hips, the dragon egg somehow tucked into her arm at her elbow, some kind of dragon version of carrying a baby on a mother's hip.

"We can't take them with us to Glasdon. What if they break? And Uncle Ralph's men know the value of the eggs," I worried.

Lindis could hardly stay behind and nurse Midnight back to health while guarding two eggs. Falk raised his eyebrows at me when I caught his eye. He wasn't about to play babysitter while I ran off with Grandmother into a fight.

Spark and Lindis exchanged stares. Spark wrapped his tail around my legs in his version of crossing his arms in stubborn refusal. He did pick up the dragon egg though, as if he were offering to carry it.

I had an idea. "Grandmother? What do you think?"

She knew what I meant without me even asking in dryad. "It's quite possible, yes. I can hide them and your friend Midnight."

"Spark," I said, "Can you hunt something for Midnight to eat before we go?"

Spark never needed an excuse to hunt—or eat. Those two activities topped his list of favorite pastimes. He launched himself into the surrounding woods so quickly, he was in danger of recreating the vortex I had caused when growing too fast.

"What are we going to do about him?" Grandmother asked, waving her arm at Brandon. "I'm not working my magic with him standing there."

As one, our eyes found the stranger in our midst. "We can't trust him," I said.

"Of course you can," Brandon argued. "I'm generally loyal to those I work for, although that policy needs careful review after this disaster." He shrugged. "And I owe you. I'll guard the eggs and your back while you rescue the girl."

Lindis hissed. Falk grunted. But Grandmother, she chuckled. "You won't be able to find them after I'm done."

I touched her arm. Silently I asked, "Are you strong enough to command the woods, after what you have been through?"

She answered out loud. "Are you kidding? You gave me enough power to last me several weeks. The trees are still alive with it. They're so grateful, they won't need but a suggestion from me."

And so it was that the group was privileged to see a real dryad in action. Even I was left in awe, and I had some idea of what was to come.

Chapter 30

My simple dryad tricks were nothing compared to Grandmother's talent. She commanded a labyrinth of trees to surround the eggs. The effort seemed almost a shame given that Midnight had just spent a day finding and digging them up, but it had to be done.

Roots slithered in a whirl of motion, creating an underground grotto, reminding me of Redwood's cavern. A shaft of sunlight shown directly into the opening, which was just large enough for Midnight. He gave a tired grunt, accepted the eggs and hopped in amongst the soft grasses and curled his tail around himself.

The greenery blurred then. Mushrooms in gold and white lined up across trunks like little soldiers. Lattice-shaped red ones emitted the fetid odor of a decaying body.

"The mushrooms are poisonous in case you wondered," she told the group. "Don't step on them. Breathing the spores can be dangerous."

Grandmother had better make it back here alive or those eggs were as good as stuck there because I certainly couldn't untangle the mass of magic she created. In two blinks it was as though we had been transported to another forest altogether.

"No food, no welcome mat, no shelter," her dryad sang. The trees responded, morphing from huge and healthy to a twisted tangle of creaking branches. Poison oak shot up along one edge of the enclave. A nearby white walnut half fell, looking like it could completely topple and crush anyone who dared squeeze underneath the looming trunk. Vines dangled within darker corners of brush. They had an uncanny resemblance to snakes.

"So if I should ever come across a dangerous patch of woods, should I search for treasure?" Brandon actually had a glint of humor in his eyes.

"Be my guest," Grandmother invited.

"Hmm." He leaned against his Ice Maiden. "Perhaps some other time."

Spark reappeared with three rabbits and half a deer. He paced in front of the tangle, looking for an entrance. He snorted and raised his snout, sniffing. Finally he dove forward into the bushes, rattling branches and calling for Midnight.

A few minutes later he appeared around a broad swath of messy growth. He could smell Midnight easily enough, even considering the bloody catch he carried, but despite scurrying to and fro, he would disappear around one side of a tree only to pop back up coming from another direction a few seconds later.

After he gulped down an entire squirrel in frustration, Grandmother spoke another command.

"Try again now," I instructed.

He toddled off and this time, in between one waving bush and the next, he was completely enveloped by the underbrush. His grunting went oddly quiet. Where he had rustled the underbrush during his earlier search, this time, silence swallowed him whole.

"If a man were in there," Brandon said, "or for that matter, the dragonkin that is resting within, can he find his way out?"

As if on command, Spark reappeared, hopping down from a large branch. He was no worse for the wear, and not at all worried.

"Would you care to try?" Grandmother answered Brandon with a sly smile.

He met her gaze and then stepped closer, squinting at the looming darkness. He touched the thick bark of the outermost tree, but pulled away fast when a large hornet appeared from a cavity and began buzzing around his head. "Ah well, I've work to find to make my living. If you've no use for the horses, I'll be on my way."

Lindis stalked up to him. "Not so fast. We don't require them at the moment, but it would behoove you to wait for us in Glasdon. We might yet need them."

She didn't bother to step back before turning dragon. She was intimidating as a human. Going full dragon that close to a person could send him screaming, but Brandon stood his ground and said quietly, "Stand. Be still," to his horses. His Ice Maiden lifted her head, but was soothed instantly by his voice. The other two tried to rear back, but calmed with another command from him.

"I can carry two for now," Lindis belted out in her gravelly voice. "Boost your grandmother up," she ordered.

I didn't need to be told twice.

* * *

Lindis had been to Glasdon before and even better, at least for us, she had been to the church and inside of it.

"I'll drop you near the church door. Get to the bell tower at the back of the church. There's a window on the outside wall with a clear view. I wasn't up there, but Zoe shot arrows into the nave from there so there's also an opening that overlooks the inside of the church."

As plans went, it sounded simple. That worried me greatly.

The church was perched on the edge of a cliff near the pinnacle of a steep mountain. After the very first pass around, it was obvious the plan wouldn't work.

No wonder Uncle Ralph had deposited Ava and Prince Irwin there. His two top men could probably hold the church against a seige with no help. Given the crossbows aimed at us from near the back door, Uncle hadn't relied on only using two men either. There were the two at the door and, no doubt, there was at least one more guard inside with the prisoners.

The crosswinds above the natural land barrier tried to upend Lindis before we finished our first circle. "Damn, the crossbows!" she hissed.

There was no time for a reply. I was too busy grappling for a better hold against her slippery scales as she twisted.

Her glide down had been easy, but as she battled to climb, wind buffeted us from more than one direction.

"Hang on!" She dove again, getting under the worst draft, but her move drew fire from the crossbows below.

My knees clenched tight, but I slid anyway. Desperate, I hooked my fingers around her wing to keep from tumbling off.

Grandmother yelped, one leg hitting me as the arrow swooshed by.

Lindis yanked up out of the dive and beat her wings hard. Spark squawked encouragement from high above us. Then again, he might be cauterwauling a protest against the gusts that were attempting to knock him head over tail.

Lindis fought for altitude, turning, gliding and then working her wings hard. Blue sky flashed by my eyes, followed by a roof, rocks and then more sky.

Sucking in air as though I were the one flying, I locked my knees down and grabbed dragon parts with both hands. Grandmother scrabbled for a hold behind me just as desperately. Lindis had flown carefully before, always aware of her burden. We didn't have that luxury this time.

She rolled and halted, then dove.

Grandmother slammed into me. I twisted and grabbed her tunic. That delayed her slide, but barely. She snaked out a limb and locked it around one of the horns that grew out of Lindis' tail.

"Okay?" I gulped.

Grandmother nodded, breathing so hard she didn't bother to speak aloud. Her dryad stuttered in my head. "...taking a...horse next time! Scales...sharp." She shook a bloody hand and glared at me.

Grandmother stayed nearly lying down wrapped around the horn as I turned back around.

Lindis circled again, flying high above the reach of arrows. Falk flew alongside and perched lightly in front of me. "I'll dive under the crossbow fire and into that back window."

"I'm dropping these two at the base of the mountain," Lindis said. "I can't break into the front window with them on my back."

"The tower," Grandmother yelled.

I swallowed and dared another dizzy peek below. The bell tower was at the rear of the church. The archers were below it, waiting at large double doors. If Lindis dropped us anywhere on the roof or tower, we could crawl in around the bell.

"Drop us on the bell tower," I shouted.

"The opening isn't big enough," Falk said. "The bell is in the way."

If she didn't land us somewhere soon, we'd fall off anyway.

"We can't get in as humans," I yelled at Lindis, "But we can get in."

Her happy cackle came with a lick of flame. "You're on." She dipped low. "Hang on tight. Going down fast."

She could have given us a few seconds to adjust. Falk had to dive off or be stuffed into my face. I jammed my legs into the shoulders of her wings and closed my eyes. Grandmother yelped from behind me, but she had been wrapped pretty tightly around that horn, and she wasn't likely to let loose for even a second.

The dive wasn't nearly as steep as the first one, but the bell tower came up fast. Lindis approached it from the cliffside to avoid the archers.

As soon as I saw the roof, I readied myself to jump, but Lindis actually touched down on the pitch, letting me leap and straddle the center. I reached back to help Grandmother, but she was already next to me, holding on to the corner of the bell tower with one hand and balancing her feet on the ridge.

"Let's go." Grandmother was already changing. Her roots and branches twisted into the openings in the tower, diving around the bell.

I crawled closer, wondering what would happen if someone rang the bell. Would it snap off one of my branches?

Lindis launched back into the air, roaring a battle cry. The bellow echoed across the valley, bouncing. She was one dragon, but she managed to sound like twenty. Smart Glasdon residents dove for cover inside buildings with strong roofs overhead. I was a friend, but the challenge still sent a primal warning down my spine.

The roof was made of flat fired tiles. It was very slippery.

Ignoring the danger, I squeezed my pack past the bell, letting it dangle down into the tower, and then I began to change. Although there was sunshine, there was no ground, no soil. The wind sucked my breath away almost before my lungs could capture the air.

My roots headed down, looking for the comfort of soil. They wouldn't find it in the cold stones of the church, but down was the right direction anyway.

Chapter 31

Grandmother screamed. Incongrously, I heard the thunk of a hard object hitting solid wood after her protest. We weren't touching, but a vibration of pain channeled along my fibers.

I stuffed myself around the bell so quickly, the walls blurred as one sense changed to another. The tower was barely large enough for a human. The tunnel leading down housed nothing more than dust and a sketchy rope ladder.

Over the years, parts of the ladder had been reinforced with chunks of wood here and there, but most of it was of questionable use. A very desperate or skilled individual could use the stone holds and ladder together to stay perched long enough to ring the bell or perhaps chase bats out when they became too entrenched.

Grandmother's roots had been stretched along the tunnel as she grew downward, but now they were shrinking away too fast. I felt her changing to human.

Her dryad sent a message of anger and pain mixed with worrisome flashes of encroaching darkness. A dagger quivered from her main trunk where she had halted halfway down below me.

Almost before I could grasp what I had seen, she was yanked sideways into an opening barely large enough to fit her rapidly changing form.

"Oh no!"

I wrapped my roots around the ladder, grabbed my pack from where it was wedged above and shifted to fully human. I kept the pack in front of my face to block the smoke that suddenly wafted upwards. Whoever waited in the alcove had ignited the dangerous dragonsbane and dryad mix. The tunnel was a perfect smoke stack.

I'd made it for a long time without relying on my dryad. If it went missing now, I wasn't about to let it slow me down.

Holding my breath, I slung the pack around. One hand grabbed the ladder, the other held my dagger. I aimed for the opening.

It was easy to miss. The ladder continued straight down to the church floor, but I wanted to pop into the room halfway to the bottom.

I swung my legs down, kicking before finding more ladder. I dropped my handful of rope and dove for the opening, twising into a roll.

Glass shattered in a magnificent explosion that echoed through the church. Glass? Either the walls were vibrating, or I'd hit harder than planned. But I didn't feel any cuts.

I slashed wildly with my dagger, not seeing the source of the glass, but not caring. The alcove that Lindis had told us about was, indeed, the perfect place to keep watch. Saul and Jake, Uncle's top thugs, had noticed and taken up residence. When Grandmother in dryad form had snaked past the opening, they instantly knew the danger.

Saul had Grandmother wrestled to the ground, but her teeth were latched onto his ear. What was left of it was likely deaf from her screeched threats. Blood spattered across the floor, some from the ear and some from where Saul or Jake had stabbed her.

No one was expecting me. Nor were any of us expecting Falk. He came diving in the outside window, landing in a half crouch, his sword out and swinging.

I raced to help Grandmother, trying to miss her and stab Saul, but the two of them slammed into a wall and then rolled back at me. I finally settled on changing my arm to a chunk of branch. What was good enough for Uncle Ralph was bound to be good enough for his men.

For years Saul and Jake had taken turns making snide comments and rude noises whenever they knew we were listening. They followed Ava and me, and they harassed Grandmother at every turn, all with Uncle Ralph's blessing.

I clubbed Saul over the head. The resounding *thwack* was gratifying, but there was no rest yet. I hopped over the two still rolling forms, ready to swing again, but the blow must have stunned Saul nearly immobile because Grandmother slammed her knee into his groin.

If his high-pitched squeak was any indication, she must have retained some ability to call her dryad because it appeared that after her knee scored a hit, branches were now trying to yank off body parts.

I put him out of his misery by smacking his head again. Whirling and ready to extract more revenge, this time on Jake, I lifted my weapon to find only Falk. He stared at a pair of fingers clinging to the outside window.

"Oh, good," I panted. "You pushed him out?"

Falk smiled an evil smile. "He leapt past me for his freedom, and then tried to change his mind halfway out when he decided the drop was too far."

"Typical. Jake never was any good at original thought. Always had to be told what to do, and he screwed that up too." I took my club arm over to the window and slammed it down.

Jake didn't even bother to scream. It was more like a long whine that ended with an abrupt grunt.

I spun back around. Without concentration, my arm changed back. Falk reached for my hand and lifted my fingers to his lips.

"Bravo."

He did not release my fingers as we hurriedly joined Grandmother at the inside window that looked down over the nave.

The source of the broken glass became instantly clear. There was a dragon sitting in the aisle. She had quite obviously come in through the stained glass window over the altar. Spark guarded her back from atop a stone angel statue.

Those two dragons sure knew how to clear a room.

Chapter 32

Standing near the altar, Prince Irwin was bound as tightly as any prisoner of war. Ropes secured his wrists, and thicker ones were wrapped around his entire body. He must have cursed his captors because his mouth was sealed with at least two layers of cloth.

Ava was bound as well, but they had run out of rope. She was held secure with various pieces of cloth and leather strips, at least two of which looked as though they had been torn from Prince Irwin's royal green and gold tunic.

At twelve years of age, Ava had learned to turn one hand into a branch with twigs. Many times in the last year and a half, she had expressed fear that she would never be able to progress beyond that point. She'd mope about, her head hanging off one side of the bed. "Failure. I am nothing more than a handful of twigs."

"Grandmother says that once you show a sign of talent, it is only a matter of practice and time," I'd tell her patiently.

"What if she is wrong?"

"Uncle says that no man wants a wooden woman. I suppose you could win the highest of princes if you are unable to become a tree."

I winced now at the memory of those teasing words. She was laid out near the altar like a prize.

I reached to ask Grandmother if she was alright, but she was already on the ladder leading down into the church.

"Hurry up, we must free Ava!" she shouted back at us. Her shoulder was bloody from what had been a deep wound, but it was scabbing over already.

By the time we reached the floor of the church, Grandmother was halfway up the aisle. Lindis had gone human. Spark was behind Ava, working at her ties with his teeth.

Lindis slashed the prince free with one hand turned claw. "I swear, if you don't get married soon, Prince, we dragons will lock you up. You cannot keep kidnapping young girls in the hopes of finding one who will have you."

Prince Irwin croaked a protest.

She shrugged off his defense. "I care not that you had nothing to do with the actual kidnapping. You aren't married. Fix it." She had his tunic wrapped in one dragon fist now. The prince was not a small man, but Lindis was not a dragon to be messed with, whether in human form or not.

He managed to keep his feet and a steady stare.

As soon as Grandmother and Spark freed Ava, I gave my sister a fierce hug and a waterskin. She took three giant swallows and then kindly handed it to Prince Irwin.

Without taking his eyes from Lindis, Prince Irwin gratefully drank. He spat the first two sips off to the side and then swallowed the rest of the water. He coughed twice before saying, "Nice to see you again, Dragon. Lindis, isn't it?"

In disgust, Lindis released him and stepped back. "Nice to see me? I would think you'd had more than enough of us. If you'd marry, these unpleasant circumstances would cease."

He gave a half courtly bow and nearly toppled over. One shaking hand darted out to the altar to save himself. "Ah, I wouldn't miss the beauty of your presence for any reason. That can certainly be the only reason I made the wise decision to kidnap an underaged girl and appear so close to your territory."

Lindis glared at him ferociously for a moment, but then she blinked. She pursed her lips in indecision. Perhaps she respected sarcasm. Or maybe, given that she was a dragon, sparring was her way of showing affection. "I will not rescue you from your foolishness again, Prince."

His eyebrows quirked with humor. "I shall endeavor to find myself a wife quickly."

"At the very least find someone who can guard you better than you've managed thus far."

The prince smiled and he dared, he actually had the audacity, to sweep her with a speculative glance. "Not a job for the faint of heart or one without a special cache of weapons. I do believe you are onto something. It will take a very special someone to guard my person."

Her eyes narrowed suspiciously before she turned and stalked to the back of the church, except because she was a dragon, her gait was more of a graceful glide.

Ava was propped against Spark, who happily kept her standing. Her brown hair was tangled and looked as though a large chunk was missing, but her hazel eyes were bright and shining with tired determination.

I gave her another long squeeze, interrupting Grandmother who was bringing her up to date on who, why and how we had managed to arrive in time. "How are you holding up?" I asked.

She accepted cheese from my hand, but sidled a guilty glance at the prince.

I smiled. "Let me guess. You gave him a very difficult time of it after you were kidnapped."

"I thought he was responsible!"

I handed the prince some food. "She's worth her weight in gold," I told him.

He nodded, and his blue eyes twinkled. "And if you think to sleep on her watch, she is likely to stab your eyes out if she finds a nearby stick. She'll also happily eat all the food available if you don't eat your share quickly."

I don't think he meant to admit he had sacrificed his own share of food in order to make sure she had enough, but I suspected that is what he alluded to. "Thank you," I said softly.

His eyes dropped to the cheese. After eating it and accepting more water, he returned his attention to Lindis.

She glared back at him, but with less hostility now that there was some distance between them.

"Any chance you can help me return home?" he asked.

Since the question was directed at her, no one else answered.

"Is that the best place for you?" she finally demanded.

Giving in to exhaustion, he sat rather suddenly very near my feet. "Perhaps a vacation is in order."

Falk's eyes followed his every move. He didn't step closer, nor did he let down his guard.

I grinned at him and then handed off the store of food to Ava to sort out.

It felt odd to think I might belong next to him rather than Ava and Grandmother, but I followed my instinct to stand near him.

He stopped frowning as soon as I sidled close. More worrisome, his eyes lit up. "It would be a good idea if your grandmother met Redwood before she returned to Anton. Don't you think?"

Grandmother studied Falk from head to toe, her sharp gaze critical and slightly accusatory.

I waved my hand, but there would be no relief from the tension until she had made up her mind about him. "Redwood is magnificient," I agreed. "Falk lives there, and honestly, I've never met anyone like Redwood. He knows everything there is to know about Falk and the surrounding forest." Did Falk realize that Grandmother would be able to extract his every secret?

Falk acknowledged my words with a bow in her direction. "Redwood is likely to welcome you as heartily as your granddaughter was welcomed by both of us."

Ava asked, "But what about the prince? We can't leave him here."

Falk sighed. "The prince may as well come along too. We can hardly allow him to return to Anton—"

"To be kidnapped again," Lindis put in. "I will not take you back just yet, Prince. Not until I've taught you a technique or two to defend yourself.

You can stay with the dragons."

My heart beat faster. "We aren't going back to Uncle," I told Grandmother.

Grandmother put her hand over mine. It was a neat trick considering I was too far for a human arm to have reached. "We don't need charity, child. I still have your father's fortune."

I met her eyes. "Unless you have a place picked out, we need to be safe." It was not exactly a declaration on my part, but Falk helped.

He rested his arm across my shoulders. "She is safe with me. You are welcome in my home."

My face blushed fiercely, and...oh, who was I kidding. I was happier tucked under his arm than I'd ever been in my life. When I made no move to extract myself, he pulled me closer still.

My grandmother's eyes twinkled. "She may be safe with you, but you may be taking on more than you imagine. Perhaps it's time someone other than a frail old lady ran after her trying to keep her out of trouble." She offered a hand, one that was not frail in the least, to Falk.

He accepted it and helped her step down from the raised dais.

"Well, then. Let's go visit this interesting Redwood and see what stories it has to tell," she said.

Falk offered her his free arm. I was already perched on his other side. Spark wedged himself under Ava's arm. She leaned against the dragonkin happily. Her legs might tingle from lack of circulation, but otherwise, she appeared to be healthy and in one piece.

We swept down the church aisle. The thought of calling where we were headed "home" didn't feel quite right, but the future certainly shone with a brighter edge than it had when I first left Anton.

At the door, Falk extracted himself and checked outside carefully even though Lindis had already walked out.

He remained blocking the doorway until I pushed against his back. Only then did he let me squeeze through.

My eyes quickly searched under the window for Jake. There was a smear of disturbed gravel. On the stone entryway where we now stood, there was a suspicious bloody spot and a broken arrow.

Brandon waited patiently a few steps away with five horses in tow. "Your uncle's men had other places to be. Left in a right hurry, they did."

From behind me Grandmother said, "I guess you didn't offer them a horse to make their journey easier."

He smiled. "I didn't know how many you'd be needing. Seemed a shame to run short after coming all this way. Me and the men, we had a nice chat though."

Uncle's men would have recognized Brandon. He could have walked right up to them. I scuffed at the smear of blood on the stones. It had soaked in so there was nothing more than an ugly blotch.

I poked Falk. "When you came in the window, did you have to worry about the archers?"

"Nope."

"Well," Grandmother said, "This will certainly beat traveling by dragon."

Ava snorted. "No way." She eyed Spark, but I shook my head.

"Not yet. But he might get large enough. He eats enough to double his size every other day."

Lindis grunted. "I was planning on dangling the prince from my claws all the way home. Too bad you showed up with horses."

Brandon stepped forward with one of the mounts, offering the reins to Grandmother. "M'lady?"

Grandmother gave him a raised brow. I thought she might refuse, but she finally accepted the reins.

"What has she against traveling by dragons?" Ava asked. "I would dearly love to fly!"

"It's a long fall, is all," I replied, boosting her up onto another of the horses.

Since we were short a mount, I assumed Falk would fly back with Lindis. He did change to hawk, but as soon as I was mounted, he settled on my shoulder.

I beamed and changed all of my upper arm to bark so he wouldn't have to be so careful with his claws. Glad that he had decided to stay with us near the ground, I rubbed my head against his soft feathers.

He leaned into me and clucked sweet nothings loud enough for only me to hear.

Finally. Now I was home.

Other Works

The Moon Shadow series is contemporary urban fantasy (**Under Witch Moon, Under Witch Aura, Under Witch Curse, and Ghost Shadow**). Adriel is an earth witch working hard to make an honest living. When she finds herself on the wrong end of black magic—it's either solve the crime or die trying.

The Sedona O'Hala series (**Executive Lunch, Executive Retention, Executive Sick Days, Executive Dirt**) is a series of humorous cozy mysteries: Sedona must solve a few crimes while fighting her way up the corporate ladder; mostly she dangles from her fingertips just trying to survive.

One Good Eclair (A Nutrition Mafia Mystery) is a zany mystery tale full of intrigue and laughs. Can Ivy cook her way out of her mafia uncle's latest mess?

Catch an Honest Thief is a stand alone mystery, combining a stealthy caper in the New Mexico desert with high-tech gadgets. Alexia must try to save her career—and her life.

Dragons of Wendal, a fantasy adventure, is the first in this series. Zoe intends to learn magic, but the mages at the university might not be willing to teach her what she needs to know. **Fairy Bite** is book three in the series.

Soul of the Desert is a historical adventure of a boy on the run from the mafia. Which is worse, the guns of New York or the dangerous desert of New Mexico?

Tracking Magic (Max Killian Investigations), Sage, and Black-Tie Bingo are all adventure-filled anthologies. You might also enjoy **Year of the Mountain Lion**, a short story available in ebook form only.

Visit Maria at: www.BearMountainBooks.com.

www.ingramcontent.com/pod-product-compliance
Lightning Source LLC
Chambersburg PA
CBHW021045130626
46552CB00005B/2021